Sussex Folk Tales for Children

Xanthe Gresham Knight

and Robin Knight

Illustrated by Sherry Robinson

This book is dedicated to Paula Cox, who always made the space to

listen to stories and share them gently on her travels.

First published 2018

The History Press
The Mill, Brimscombe Port
Stroud, Gloucestershire, GL5 2QG
www.thehistorypress.co.uk

British Library Cataloguing in Publication Data.
A catalogue record for this book is available from the British Library.

ISBN 978 0 7509 8426 3

Typesetting and origination by The History Press
Printed and bound by CPI Group (UK) Ltd

Contents

About the Authors and Illustrator

ROBIN KNIGHT is a poet, freelance journalist and novelist and has lived in various parts of Sussex for decades. He has walked, ridden, cycled or driven over almost every inch of the terrain in these stories.

XANTHE GRESHAM KNIGHT has been a storyteller for over twenty years, and has toured the world to perform for children, adults and families. She has now come home to Sussex. These local tales and images have rooted her in the streets, downs, seas and beaches of this county. This is her first written collaboration with Sherry and Robin.

SHERRY ROBINSON is an artist and musician and has worked with Xanthe Gresham Knight on collaborative storytelling adventures for over twenty years. A lover of magic realism, Sherry has created many musical compositions in response to the rich visual images evoked by the stories. She finds drawing similar to playing a musical instrument. It is a way of entering other worlds.

Acknowledgements

Thanks to John Copper and family for the songs, all recorded in the *Copper Family Songbook*. In this collection, we have incorporated details and characters from Bob Copper's books *Early to Rise*, *A Man of no Consequence* and the prize-winning *A Song for Every Season*.

To Paula Cox (1960–2018), artist and dearest friend, with whom we spent many happy hours discussing the stories and images in this book. She had a real belief in the power of storytelling.

Thanks to Ray Williams of Blanton Museum of Art, Texas, for guidance on how to develop 'A Thimbleful of Sugar', James

Easton, Allan Davies and Philippa Tipper for 'Jack and the Devil', Des and Ali Quarrell of Mythstories Museum of Myth and Fable for the inspiration for 'Seven Sisters (and One Shepherd)'.

Thanks to www.sussexfolktalecentre. org, Brighton Libraries for the many books, including *The Wilmington Giant* by Rodney Castleden, *Folklore of Sussex* by Jaqueline Simpson, and *A Dictionary of The Sussex Dialect* by Revd W.D. Parish.

For further reading, Michael O'Leary's *Sussex Folk Tales* is a gem for both adults and children. There are some excellent storytelling clubs in Sussex – if you would like to find out more please visit:

brightonstorytellers.co.uk
guesthousestorytellers.com

Foreword by Catherine Smith

Here in Sussex, we know we're very lucky. We can run around on glittering beaches and wade into sparkling seas; we have towering white cliffs, springy green hills splodged with sheep … and lots of very odd-sounding place names. We also have plenty of stories, ancient stories that show us how Sussex was shaped, not only by the weather and the passing of time, but by people from 'elsewhere' who settled in this beautiful place. These stories show us how Sussex people used to live, and what they believed – they are special to Sussex, but also contain echoes of stories from all around the world, such as the idea of trying to fish the moon out of a pool or star sisters that land on high places to dance.

So … did you know that the name 'Sussex' came from the old word for 'South Saxons' (*Suthsaxe*)? (Imagine those Saxons: 'A band of warrior pirates from Northern Europe, who arrived on the coast like wolves among sheep.') Or that Sussex was once the smuggling capital of England?

Ever wondered how people used to travel between towns and villages, and whom they might have encountered along the way – perhaps a hard-hearted highwayman or, even worse, a phantom hard-hearted highwayman …

Ever wondered how the Seven Sisters and Devil's Dyke acquired their names?

In these extraordinary stories, you'll meet a surprising cast of characters, including the Devil himself – also known as 'Mr Lucifer', who was happily at home in Sussex until Saint Dunstan, Grannie Annie, and a clever boy called Jack set to work; a hare with magical powers; a gleeful fairy called Puck; a brave and clever girl who outsmarts smugglers to regain possession of her precious mare and foal; a terrifying butter-loving giant made of bread … you'll meet centaurs, dancers, shepherds and abandoned children. They all have wonderful stories to tell you.

Catherine Smith

CATHERINE SMITH lives in Lewes and is a writer of poetry, fiction, Live Literature and radio drama. She teaches for The Creative Writing Programme in Brighton, The Arvon Foundation and The Poetry School.

Introduction

Although I'm not rich and although I'm not poor,
I'm happy as those that's got thousands or more.

Folk song from the *Copper Family Songbook*

Like songs, stories are jewels, mined from the hearts of storytellers and the earth beneath their feet. Every time you tell a tale or sing a song to someone else, it shines a little brighter.

Particularly, the Copper family of Rottingdean have shared with us their Sussex riches: songs and stories collected over hundreds of years. John Copper, born in 1949, learned songs at the knee of his grandfather, Jim. As the family rehearsed, he kept young

John interested by hiding a tube of smarties somewhere on his person and helping the lad search through his pockets:

'Let's hev a look in this 'un, young brancher, shall us? Doh, 'tent in there noither!'

The smarties were always in the last pocket.

Folk tales, too, are handed down from generation to generation. We hope that you will pass them on, and in so doing, find the smarties in the pocket of each.

Xanthe and Robin

1

The Chalk Giant – How Stories Came to Sussex

◎ Wilmington ◎

When spring comes in the birds do sing,
The lambs do skip and the bells do ring …

Old Jack Pettit's Song –
farmworker of Rottingdean

Before the first flints were struck to make a fire, before the first stories were told to warm the heart and before the seasons came to Sussex, there lived a girl giant and a boy giant who were brother and sister.

The girl was called Shine because the second she was born, the sun rose, and wherever she went, the sun followed. Whether Shine got her sparkle from the sun, or whether the sun got its sparkle from Shine, no one knew.

The boy was called Dum because the first time he opened his mouth it was to sing:

Dum de dum diddle
Rol me rol riddle
Skip de skip skiddle.

Shine ran from east to west over the grass and shingle collecting things to share with her brother in the evening: crab apples, thyme-scented honey, sheep's teeth and tusks. She kept them in a heap in the corner of their cave.

Dum spent his days looking after the little sheep. In those days, there were thousands in these parts. They gave the giants milk, cheese and fleeces. It took about eighteen sheeps' fleeces to make a single coat for a giant.

One day, Shine found a piece of stag antler. She gave it to Dum. He made holes along the bone with a sharpened stone, put the whistle to his mouth and started to play. As he practised, the bees buzzed, the fish flipped and the leaves rustled. In those days, it was always summer.

As soon as the sun began to sink, all the other giants huddled underneath their sheepskins and went to sleep. Dum would take a soft piece of chalk and draw pictures on the rocks and Shine would say, 'Once upon a time … Once upon a time … Once upon a time …' but she could never think of what to say next. She was looking for a string of words to help her fall asleep, words that would make pictures, pictures that would make dreams.

One evening, Dum and Shine were playing hide and seek. It was Shine's turn to hide.

She ran fast around Windover Hill because at any moment Dum would be shouting, 'Coming ready or not!' She stopped abruptly. There was a gate in the grass in the side of the hill. It had two posts on either side and two doors that met in the middle. She pushed and they creaked apart, but just a chink. Whether in those days gates spoke when they creaked, or whether giants could understand the language of doors, I don't know, but this is what it said:

Give me a gift to enter in
And 'Once upon a time' begins.

There's fire below, and tales unheard
They lie in wait, each spark a word.

But once the words begin to burn
The fire keeper can't return.

Shine had no idea what 'fire' was, but she longed for a story. 'Please have this,' she said to the door. Pulling off her hat made from the bark of the silver birch, she threw it into the darkness in front of her.

The door opened and she passed through. Seeing a white path hugging the inside of the hill she began to walk and the gate closed behind her. It was dark, but Shine could find her steps by following the ribbon of white chalk, which spiralled down until she came to another gate. She pushed. It creaked like the first one:

A gift will cause these gates to part
Then 'Once upon a time' can start.

Shine was excited, how she longed for a story! She took off her necklace of oyster shells and threw it into the darkness. The gate opened. She passed through it and carried on walking down the winding path.

At the following five gates, Shine gave away:

her snakeskin belt,

her prized white feather,

her favourite stone with the hole in the middle,

her bracelet of walnut shells,

and finally, her cloak of many sheepskins.

She shivered, but not for long because behind the seventh door was a pile of flints and dry branches.

Shine got an idea. She picked up one stone and struck it against the other. It sparked! Shine struck again but this time she held the spark against the wood and fire flashed. Red and orange flames warmed her cold bones. The Hill seemed to sigh a happy sigh and soon Shine knew why. In the crackle she heard words:

Once upon a time, in a land between the hills and the sea …

While Shine was listening to the world's first story, Dum was searching for her. He tried all their secret places but she was nowhere to be found. He was so unhappy he couldn't sing a song or play a note. Without his music, the bees stopped buzzing, the fish stopped flipping and the leaves fell off the trees. Without Shine's sparkle, bit by bit, day by day, the sun lost its strength. It rose late and sank early. Every day it became weaker. The giants became weak with cold and hunger. Dum stared at the sea. He couldn't move for sadness.

Then, one morning, he heard a rapping in his heart like a knocking on a door. 'Ready or not! Come and find me!' It was Shine's voice. Only he could hear it. He was on his feet running just as he had months ago during their game of hide and seek. He could feel her speaking to him, 'Cold, really cold!' He came to Windover Hill, 'Warm! Getting warmer! Hot! Burning hot!'

The grass parted and Dum saw a double gate. It had two posts on either side and two doors that met in the middle. He pushed and they creaked apart, but just a chink:

> *A song will open up these gates*
> *Inside your sister Shine awaits.*
>
> *And once the singer is inside*
> *It's no more seek; it's no more hide.*
>
> *Once the seeker enters in*
> *The Hill will make him sing and sing.*

Dum sang:

> *Rol me rol riddle*
> *Skip de skip skiddle.*

Dum de dum diddle
Whistle me whistle.

The gate opened, Dum took out his bone flute and walked through. As it closed behind him, he started to follow the same path that Shine had taken, playing all the while. Each time he came to a gate, it opened.

When he was through the seventh gate, he saw Shine sitting beside a fire. Amazed by the blaze, he stopped playing. In the crackling flames he heard, 'Once upon a time in a place between the hills and the sea …' but Dum shut his ears to the rest. He could see Shine's eyes were misty; she was far away in another world. She looked thin and tired and her sparkle had dimmed. He must get her back into the sun. She needed it, and it needed her.

'Shine!'

As if coming up from the bottom of a well, Shine gasped for air and blinked, her eyes snapping into focus.

'Dum! Where have I been?'

Dum explained that she had been lost for months, that without her the sun was dying and the giants were cold and starving.

Shine was on her feet. 'Let's go home. Now!'

But as they pushed the gate to begin the journey upwards, it creaked:

> *The hill is lonely, both can't go*
> *Send Shine above, leave Dum below.*
>
> *Then Shine can share the stories learned*
> *And save the sun on her return.*
>
> *The tales can go where tales belong*
> *But shepherd stay and sing your song.*

Shine returned to the daylight alone with her pockets full of flints and her heart full of stories. As soon as the sun saw her, it started to beam. Down in the cave, Dum played his whistle and sang his songs to the fire and the darkness.

Whistle me whistle
Dum de dum diddle.

Rol me rol riddle
Skip de skip skiddle.

His notes vibrated up through chalk and flint and as they bounced off the rock, they increased in volume so that in the world outside the hill, the water caught the rhythm and started to burble, the wind whistled, the bees buzzed and the birds copied his melodies. Spring had come and once more everything was singing Dum's song. The giants found themselves humming along, harmonising and making up their own tunes.

That evening, Shine struck the two flints together and for the first time the giants had fire.

They gathered round and Shine began to tell all the stories she had learned when she was inside the hill.

After six months, once the trees had fruited, Shine decided it was time to return

to Dum. She took a basketful of apples, wild strawberries, mulberries, elderberries, hazelnuts, walnuts and honey. The seven gates of Windover Hill opened at her offerings. Brother and sister hugged each other and shared their news, then Shine sat beside the fire and Dum took the chalky path upwards.

Every year, Dum and Shine swapped places. When Shine came out of the hill it was spring and summer, when Dum returned, autumn and winter.

The winters were hard. Dum stood, hands against the gateposts of Windover Hill, waiting for Shine to call him, 'Ready or not! Come and get me!' Seeing him standing there, the hungry giants took heart. They remembered that winter never lasts – Dum would soon fetch Shine out of the hill.

As the years passed, the giants began to get tired. Dum and Shine felt that their work was done, the pattern of summer and winter had been firmly established. The next race, that of human beings, was waiting to take their place. It was time for them to go.

Dum carved an outline of himself, back against the grass, hands against the gateposts, into the chalk of Windover Hill, as a reminder that the cold of winter is always followed by the warmth of spring. Then he, Shine and all the giants gathered together the new race of people and, beside a blazing fire, passed on their songs and stories. When that was done, the giants melted into the rocks and rivers and Dum and Shine journeyed the spiralling white path inside the Hill. Each time they passed through a gate, it shut, never to open again. Brother and sister curled up like dormice and fell asleep beside the fire.

The new race passed on the songs and stories to their children and their children's children. And every story that you will ever hear, every song that you will ever sing, is an echo of those very first songs and stories. Sing them, tell them – all the hills are listening!

2

The Devil and St Dunstan

◉ Mayfield ◉

How many miles to Babylon?
Three score and ten.
Can I get there by candle-light?
Yes, and back again.
If your heels are nimble and light,
You may get there by candle-light.

Traditional poem

The Devil called Sussex his home. Here he felt his skills were appreciated. He could make the fields wave with golden corn, the sea churn with silver fish and the sun break through the clouds.

People treated him with respect.

Farmers tipped their hats, 'Mr Lucifer, you burnish* nicely – bring your fiddle to our festival!'

Fishermen whistled, 'Brother Beelzebub, you're a bettermost* sort of chappie – no flies on you!'

Sailors sang, 'Mr Diabolas we're Dutch Cousins.* Cheers!'

But churches were being built, and with the building of churches came changes. Nobody danced beneath a midnight moon, nobody raised their tankards to a whisky-wet dawn. Everybody went to bed early to be up for Sunday Mass.

One morning, the Devil stood outside Mayfield Church, a little wooden building with a crooked spire, and asked himself, 'What is that boring, drawling, moaning coming from inside? Is that supposed to be singing?'

Curious, he stood there picking the fleas from his tail and plucking the gravel from his hooves.

The singing stopped and his folk – farmers, fishermen and sailors – tumbled out down the path and into the sunshine. The Devil bounded to meet them but they ducked their heads and turned aside as a baldy old man in a brown robe with a rope around his waist came striding towards him holding a cross.

'Now, now, Old Nick, Old Scratch, Mr Grim, you listen to me! I am St Dunstan of Mayfield and I command you! Away!'

The Devil had never heard himself addressed in such a fashion. Old Nick? Old Scratch? He wasn't old! He didn't have a single white whisker. Mr Grim? Only last night he had laughed so hard and so high he shattered the windows of Telscombe Manor.

'I can see I'm not wanted!' he huffed, and left.

That night he returned to Mayfield, leaned his hairy back against the church, puffed himself up till he was as tall as the crooked spire, lifted his elbows, thrust them back and crack! The church splintered and fell.

But St Dunstan was a builder and a blacksmith as well as a saint and the next day he rolled up his brown sleeves, hauled bricks, forged iron and made the grey-stoned, red-roofed church, St Dunstan's, which still stands in Mayfield High Street today.

The Devil was cross. His horns, his hooves and everything in between tingled like a match, the second before it bursts into flame.

He decided to give St Dunstan a scare. He shaved his furry face, powdered his cheeks, reddened his lips and sprayed himself with perfume. Then he put on a pretty straw hat to cover his horns, a pretty long dress to hide his furry legs, and laced a pretty pair of boots around his hooves. As he tottered towards Mayfield, he picked a big fat flower.

She/he knocked at St Dunstan's forge and peeped round the door.

St Dunstan was looking very serious. He was sweating from the fire and his brow was black with smoke.

'Hello, Mr Thaint,' lisped the Devil in a high girly voice. 'Would you pleathe thing me a likkle thong? I do tho love your thinging! Pleathe! A hymn!'

St Dunstan saw the pretty girl and put down his tongs. 'Of course, child! Sit down.'

The Devil sat down and crossed her pretty boots.

St Dunstan cleared his throat and began to sing in a slow serious voice that went on and on and on. And on.

Soon the Devil was bored. 'Stop it!' he shouted. He threw off his hat, wiped off his lipstick, ripped off his dress and ran towards St Dunstan holding the big, fat flower in front of his eyes just as St Dunstan had held the cross that Sunday morning.

'Now you listen to me old holy sock, stop your monkey business. I am the Devil of Sussex and I command you! Away!'

The Devil began to puff himself up into the scariest shape he could think of: flaming red skin, flapping red wings, sharp red teeth and a tail that split into a thousand forks.

But St Dunstan didn't move. He smiled a slow, smug smile and began,

'Now, now …'

'Don't! Now! Now! Me!' shouted the Devil. 'I'll smash your church into rubble!'

With a '**Roooooooooar!**' he ran out the door. St Dunstan followed, grabbing a pair of red-hot tongs from his forge. As the Devil leaped towards the church, St Dunstan leaped towards the Devil and before he could bish, bash, bosh the church and grind it to gravel, St Dunstan clamped the blazing tongs onto the Devil's nose.

'Show your face in Sussex during daylight again and you'll be done for. The darkness is where you belong!'

'**Rooooooooooooooooooooooooooooooooooar!**' went the Devil and bounded over the black and white tudor houses of the village and across the fields, landing a mile away in a stream where he plunged his nose into the water.

'Hisssss!' went the tongs and fell into the flow.

Since that time it's been called the 'Roaring Stream' and sometimes it still runs red in memory of St Dunstan's iron tongs even though they didn't stay there very long, because the saint, ever thrifty, came and fetched them back.

The forge in Mayfield is now shut but St Dunstan's tongs still hang in Mayfield convent, where you can see them to this day.

* burnish – in Sussex dialect this means 'to look well'.
* bettermost – meaning 'superior'.
* Dutch Cousins – meaning 'best friends'.

3

The Secret Guardian of Sussex

◎ Rye ◎

As you've not got your cedar bow,
Your arrow and your string,
I'll fly to the top of yonder tree,
And there I'll sit and sing.

Traditional poem

The Romantic poet Robert Southey visited Rye in the summer of 1792. He stayed with his friend Tom at Mountsfield, a grand house with turrets and arched windows.

One evening, the poet was walking alone in the gardens when he came to a grove of oaks. As he pushed back the branches, he saw a pool with the full moon shining on the water.

'How darkly, deeply, beautifully blue!' he muttered poetically.

A second later he screamed and ran back through the trees, across the lawns and into the house. He burst in as dinner was being served.

'I have to tell you, Tom! The pool in your grounds … I saw a creature in it! Half beast, half man!'

'You're a poet,' said Tom affectionately, 'you imagined it!'

The young girl who was pouring the wine neither looked up nor spilled a drop. 'I don't think so, Master Tom. That'll be the Secret Guardian of Sussex. My grandma saw him once. She must have told me his story a thousand times!'

Tom moved to the fireplace, inviting the girl to sit down and tell the tale, just as her grandmother had told it. She began.

Once upon a time, Old Man Druid was walking through the forest. The wind razzed his grey curls. The sun warmed his bent back. He sang in time to the birdsong as he picked herbs for potions and berries for breakfast, putting them in a cloth bag which he wore over his shoulder:

> *Cuckoo coo,*
> *Shake the dew,*
> *Ever, ever,*
> *Ever new!*

A squirrel ran up his leg and stole a crust of bread from his pocket. When the skylark started singing, the old man laughed, waved his stick and did a crazy kick-foot dance. He was making for a special pool. He wanted to watch the moon rise in its clear waters. He wanted to be with the wild ponies and spotted deer as they came to drink. The journey would take him all day but it would be worth it. The pool had a magic that even Old Man Druid hadn't fathomed.

Many miles away, across the Downs, a hunter called Bullseye was tracking a stag with a broad back and branching antlers. It was the finest he had ever seen. All day he followed the white flashes of its tail as it bounded, making waves through the wheat fields. Although the stag's ears beat forwards and back and his nose twitched, he still hadn't smelled the hunter who trod softly, keeping the wind in his face so it would blow away his scent.

It was said of Bullseye that he could hunt using sound alone, that once he had aimed his arrow at a deer, it was as good as supper. He never missed a target. He only ever took one shot and timed it perfectly. That moment was coming; he could feel it.

The stag arrived at a pool as the sun was beginning to drop. It lowered its head to drink. On the opposite bank, Bullseye notched an arrow. Only when the stag half lifted his head and looked right at him did he fire. The arrow slammed into the trunk of an oak next to the creature, spooking it so that it galloped away. He had missed! Was it a gust of wind? Was it a trick of the light? Or was he losing his powers?

Like a cloud in the summer sky, the stag floated over fallen trees and leapt across streams, impossible to catch.

'I never miss!' The hunter beat his palm against his forehead. 'I am Bullseye! I can hit a target by sound alone!' At that moment, he heard rustling in the bushes. Determined to prove himself to himself, Bullseye snatched his bow, shut his eyes, opened his ears and fired.

Shwooooooooo – pah.

He heard it strike! A wild grey pony fell from the thicket, an arrow in her chest. From it ran a line of blood. A foal broke from the cover of the bushes to be with her mother. She nuzzled, wanting milk. The mare staggered into the pool leaving the foal at the water's edge.

Bullseye walked towards them. The foal shied. She wanted to bolt, but couldn't leave her mother behind. Not knowing how to get close without scaring off the creature, the hunter slumped on a rock. They stayed like that, with the mare in the water, the foal unable to leave, skittering beside the water's edge, Bullseye sobbing, unable to approach.

Hours passed. Looking at the moon in the water, Bullseye jumped. He'd seen the reflection of a tall man standing in silence behind him. He turned to look. The man wore a pale robe and his white hair hung to his shoulders.

Old Man Druid had arrived at the pool, but instead of seeing animals drinking peacefully, he saw only an injured mare and her broken-hearted foal.

'You deserve to cry,' he growled at Bullseye. The mare was wading deeper and deeper into the pool. The water was up to her neck now.

Bullseye lowered his head and covered his eyes.

The old man poked him with his gnarled stick, 'The question is, what will you do about it?'

'Anything. Anything to make it right!' Noting the bag of herbs across Old Man Druid's shoulder, his eyes widened. 'You're a druid, a healer! You know nature's secrets. Save the mare! Please!'

'There is only one way. And the cost to you will be great.'

'I'll do anything.'

Old Man Druid nodded. 'A life is flowing away. To save it, a life must be given. If it hadn't been for your arrow, this mare would have survived another twenty years. Will you give her twenty years of your own?'

Bullseye thought about his hut, the skins and knives, the fireplace which in winter warmed just him. He had no family. From when he opened his eyes in the morning to when he shut them at night, his only thought was of killing. 'Yes,' he replied.

Out of his bag, Old Man Druid took dried herbs and a small clay cup. He mixed the herbs with water and spoke strange words at the moon.

'Drink,' he said.

The hunter glugged the bitter, grainy contents, then wiped his mouth with the back of his hand and walked towards the mare. As he entered the water, he could feel his colour draining and his flesh melting into a white mist, which drifted towards her, pouring into her nostrils and swirling down her throat. He began to sink

Down

Down

Down

On the bank of the pool, the druid hit his stick on the ground. Bullseye's heart beat with the power of a horse. The mare began to breathe heavily and Bullseye felt her breath was his own. Clambering out of the pool, he grabbed rocks and reeds with his hands.

One leg. He was so heavy! Heave and stamp! Two legs! There was so much of him – in the pool he'd been light! Three legs? Heave and stamp! Four legs?

Bullseye looked down and saw that his chest and arms were his own, muscled and tanned, but his legs were covered with hair and hooved. He twisted round and saw that he had the body of a horse, the back legs of a horse, the swishing tale of a horse – a mare, because the little foal ran to his side and nuzzled. Bullseye was now a Centaur. He flicked his long grey tail.

Old Man Druid did a little skip. 'Well done,' he said. 'You'll have twenty years as a Centaur. You can be both mother and father to this foal.'

He opened up his cloth bag to share the last of his berries and nuts, then he, the foal and Bullseye the Centaur settled beside the pool to watch the stars.

At first light, the three of them began to wander towards the Downs. 'Let me carry that,' said Bullseye, walking alongside Old

Man Druid and taking his bag. Together they collected apples for breakfast, with the foal cantering and bucking around them.

From that day on, Old Man Druid often met up with the Centaur and his foal. They fed hungry squirrels, mended broken wings and took care of motherless cubs and calves. Sometimes they went to the little hut that had belonged to the hunter and warmed themselves by a fire. The foal grew up and had children and grandchildren so that there was often a herd of horses travelling with them.

After twenty years they returned to the pool. It reflected blue sky, gold sun, and green leaves, but only Bullseye truly understood the magic beneath the ripples.

'Are you ready to change back into a man?' asked Old Man Druid quietly.

The Centaur circled, swishing his tail. Finally, he looked into Old Man Druid's eyes.

'I am … not. I've left killing behind. I prefer to protect life. How long can I remain the secret guardian of these woods?'

Old Man Druid smiled. 'No one has ever seen a Centaur die. You can take care of Sussex for as long as there is a Sussex to take care of. But should you get tired, come back to this pool, or any pond in this county, and you'll revive!'

Having finished her story, the serving girl stood up, saying to the poet, 'That's what he was doing, Sir, refreshing himself in the pool. It's hard work being the Secret Guardian of Sussex and he's been doing it for centuries! And on that note, I'd better get on!' She began to clear away the plates, singing to herself:

> *Cuckoo coo,*
> *Shake the dew,*
> *Ever, ever,*
> *Ever new!*
>
> *Whistling swan,*
> *Skylark song*
> *On and on and*
> *On and on!*

4

Puck and the Dancing Shoes

◎ Lewes and Rottingdean ◎

The fair maid who, the first of May
Goes to the fields at break of day
And washes in dew from the hawthorn tree
Will ever after handsome be.

Traditional poem

It's me! Some call me Puck! To rhyme with luck and muck. I've bucketloads of both! I like to squelch with water beetles, fly with bats. You can't catch me! I'm the whisper in the wooded Weald, the sparkle on the sea. Some call me Pook to rhyme with spook and fluke. I'm the Ghost of the Chalk Hills, the Trickster of Tricks. I'm such a jammy dodger I always roll a six! I'm Hob to rhyme with Rob, Robin to rhyme with Goblin. I'm Robgoblin! I'm also Sprite, Fright, Tickle, Fickle, Dynamite, Meteorite, Traffic Light: alright, that's enough! Call me what you like. I've slipped on a sunbeam, skidded on the dew, run fast as a fox to be here with you to tell a true story. I'll puff it out and onto the page! May it land with a hint of lavender, a gust of sage. Here we go!

We People of the Hills keep out the way of you humans. Who knows how long you'll last? We've been here forever and will go on till never you mind, but from time to time there's one of you we take a shine to. Most of you don't see us. You only see what you expect to see and we're easy to miss. My normal height is not much taller than your middle finger. I choose speed not size, my wings are hypersonic, a shimmer behind my shoulder bones. And I'm muscled. I leap from roof to roof, tree to tree, cliff to sea. You can't catch me. Well, not normally.

I was once fond of a boy who kept his eyes open and saw me straight away. He was fast. He made a catapult from a branch of hazel and a whistle from a twig of elder. I totally trusted him until he grabbed me one afternoon as I was sunbathing on a leaf and put me in a jar with his pet insects.

I was so furious, I couldn't stop myself saying the Bigging Spell:

> Stamp one!
> Stamp two!
> I'm big
> Like YOU!

I increased in size as quick as you can flick a flick book. The jar smashed, the boy cried out, but I was gone with a whizz, like a stone shot from one of his catapults. I heard the glass cut his cheek and he bleared* for a week, which was a shame. I never went back to him again. No one pickles the Pook that is Puck! Besides, it took me days to shrink back to a size comfortable for flitting.

It wasn't long after that I met May. She was walking down Rottingdean High Street singing to herself. May was a dreamer. If I landed on her head she would take me for a Sussex Blue butterfly; if I zoomed in front of her eyes she would glint* a dragonfly. She would never put me in a jar because she didn't notice much by way of seeing, instead she loved smells and sensations.

She loved the honey-dust-hay and leather smell on the neck of the shire horse called Sultan. She loved the tang-salt, blossom-white, sea smell on the head of her baby brother Joe. And she loved to dance. 'La!'

If she had her way, she would have danced all day on the green grass of the Downs or the wet sand by the sea, because dancing – 'wheee!' – set her free. But there was work to be done, thread to be spun, clothes to wash and meals to make, but if she was awake, you can be sure this girl would shimmy, this girl would shake, even if it was only a leap between her steps or a strut at the sink.

In May's mind, there were two types of dancing – hard and soft:

Hard dancing was what May did when all the work at home and school was too much. Pent up with pirouettes she would stride up to her secret place on the Downs and begin. She danced for the hedges, the nettles and the green folds of the open hills. Up there, with the sky close, May danced as fiercely as the wind blowing over from the Isle of Wight. Her body twisted like a sugar twizzle and her eyes glittered like pear drops from the Penny Lady's sweet tray.

Soft dancing was what May called dancing with others. I often lazed on a broken branch of the rotten lime tree in the school playground while May and her friends danced in a circle, hand in hand. At those times, May's eyes were as gooey as butter fudge. She seemed to float like a piece of driftwood that thinks it's a wave.

May had one ambition. She wanted to dance in clogs, clickety, clackety, down Lewes High Street with the women and girls on May morning.

Come Christmas, May was given a brown package tied up with string. In it was a pair of clogs all the way from Lancashire. They were brown leather with white stitching and wooden soles all hammered together with nails. Her dad and eldest brother had taken on extra jobs as muck men for a season – emptying the dunnicks – the village toilets – to pay for them.

May practised her dance steps over and over. The only snag was, the clogs wouldn't soften to her feet. Her heels were covered with sores and blisters and her toenails turned black. She didn't tell anyone in case they stopped her dancing on May morning.

The night before, May was so excited she couldn't sleep a blink. She was up way before the moon went down, walking towards Mount Caburn to gather flowers. I ran with her, leap-frogging the gates and somersaulting from sheep to sheep, as the glimmer-gowks* hooted.

May was wearing her clogs, hoping that the wet grass would moisten the hard leather before the dancing started. I watched her pick and garland damp flowers in the dark. She gathered every kind of blossom, knots of lilies and handfuls of hellebore, winding them round her head, neck, wrists and ankles. As she worked, she sang:

As I walk out this May morning, this May morning so early …
I'll gather in the buds of spring before the sun comes a-rising,
With my rue-dum day, fol de riddle ray,
Wack fol de rol de riddle I-do!

May came to a circle of mushrooms as white as stars. You would call such a thing a fairy ring but we call it a dance halo. It's an overland marker of an underground ballroom where we, the People of the Hills, like to dance, especially on May's eve, when we do

it till dawn without a break, to shake awake the seeds and make them sprout.

Sometimes I'm a lazy Puck and don't want to foot it all through the night so I wasn't dancing with them – and a good job too, because May stopped gathering flowers. She put her ear to the ground. It was clear she could hear the harps harping, fiddles fiddling and whistles tooting. She began to swish and sway, then she jumped right into the ring and began to dance.

'No!' I shrieked.

She didn't hear. Her arms flicked, her hips dipped, she skipped and tripped.

'No!' But May's eyes were going melty now and I could see she felt part of everything and would jig on till sunrise!

Why shouldn't she dance? Well, I knew that beneath the halo of mushrooms, in the underground fairy ballroom, May's steps would be making the chandeliers shudder as if there was an earthquake. Fiddles would be going out of tune and the drummers wouldn't know which beat to follow. Worst of all, chalk flaking from the ceiling would be interrupting the goblins as they worked:

> Nail the leather, mend the shoe,
> In and out and pull it through,
> Stitch it, cut it, tack it, glue
> Slipper mended, lucky you.

In their dancing frenzy, the fairies need their goblin shoemakers because they wear out their footwear in hours. If the goblins lost their tempers and refused to work, the party would be over and it would all be May's fault.

'Get out of the ring!' I jumped on her shoulders and tugged at her hair. I thought she'd heard me because she stopped dancing. But no, she yawned, stretched, kicked off her clogs, curled up on her apron and fell asleep.

Once May is sleeping I've never been able to wake her even if I use my mosquito pinch.

It was then that I caught the whiff of a scent I knew so well: honeysuckle, wild rose and riverbed. The Queen of the Fairies was coming.

A mushroom fell, tipped by a bony hand that appeared from beneath the earth, followed by a silver-skinned arm and a head of dark hair crowned with spider orchids. Up she came. Her wings buzzed like a bee as she flicked her fish scale dress. The Queen of the Fairies was no taller than the distance from the earth to May's ankle bone but her voice bounced off the stars. 'Get off the roof of our ballroom!' she shrieked.

May carried on sleeping. Flushing dark as nightshade, the Queen of the Fairies scrunched up her face, opened her mouth and screamed:

Stamp one!
Stamp two!
I'm big
Like YOU!

The Queen of the Fairies erupted, stretching so tall she hit her head on the moon, then contracted until she was around May's size. In her hand was a little green bottle of cracked Venetian glass, with a tiny mirrored leaf for a stopper. The potion was a gift from the King of the Fairies. She'd had it since we rode on dinosaurs. I knew what was in it – a mixture of foxglove, hemlock and yew berry. One smear of it on May's eyes would shrink her until she was as small as a baby mouse, small enough to be pushed down a mushroom staircase into a fairy dance hall. When she woke up she would be intoxicated by the candle chandeliers, the fiddles and the drink from the buttercup punchbowl. She'd dance with the fairy folk till morning.

'What's wrong with that?' you might ask. But which morning? The fairy dance has a power that humans never understand. Their whirling plays with time like a black hole. I once lost a couple of centuries there myself. If May danced with them till morning, when she was finally pushed out, back up into the fairy halo of mushrooms, so many years would have passed there would be nothing left of Sultan, her favourite horse, but bones in the meadow. Her baby brother Joe would have died an old man a hundred years before.

The thought made me so cross I started to shout:

> Stamp one!
> Stamp two!
> I'm big
> Like YOU!

So that Puck became a bristling, brown-muscled Sprite. I stood between May and the Queen of the Fairies.

'Leave her alone!' I grabbed the Queen's wrist to stop her anointing May's eyes with her tincture. She flipped me over her shoulder and onto the grass. As she did, the Venetian glass bottle flew out of her hand and shattered on the wooden soles of May's upturned clogs, spattering them with a purple liquid. For a second we watched them sizzle.

Then:

We wrestled on the damp earth, wrestled in the dry air, on the itchy chalk. We wrestled in the soft clouds, wrestled on the wet sea, on the prickly gorse. And whether it was the wrestling that made our rage drain away, or because I'm the Queen's adopted brother and we always get bored of scrapping, we began to shrink so that it took us a few minutes to fly back to the mushroom circle. By the time we did, it was dawn and we were just in time to see May, her clogs on her shoulder skipping '*rol de riddle i do!*' down the hills towards Lewes town.

'She's gone.' I said, without looking at the Queen. 'You can carry on dancing!'

'No thanks to you!' she muttered. 'You'll pay for this!'

Brother or not, the Fairy Queen had me polishing seeds and burnishing petals for a month, but I didn't mind. The potion from the little green bottle that would have cost May so many years had just the right effect on her clogs. They shrank to fit her feet as snugly as a daffy down dilly* fits my head.

That May morning, May danced The Brighton Lasses, The Beau Knot, The Five

Knots, The Lewes Stomp and The Lacemaker. Hand in hand with the others, she was one with the street, the Downs and the whole of Lewes town.

May passed the clogs on to her daughter, who said they were far too big. But when she slipped them on, not only did they fit her like a woollen sock, they grew with her.

May's daughter didn't have a child but passed the clogs on to someone as much like her as Pook is like a sprite and Puck is like a fairy. Although that girl passed them on to her daughter, not everybody dances, so the clogs ended up in a charity box.

Last May morning, Lewes High Street was closed to traffic but open to dancers. The crowds lined the streets waiting for the May parade. They juggled their takeaway coffees with those camera phones they like to hold up at anything. In the Red Cross shop, a young girl spent all her pocket money buying May's old clogs. She put them on and whirled out of the store, her eyes sparkling like lemon sherbets, a single violet in her hair. She danced alone on the cobbles, for the dust in the sunbeams, for the clothes in the windows and for the smiles on the sea of faces.

When the other dancers skipped down from the castle, they took her hand and she danced with them, her eyes as gooey as butter fudge. As soon as one girl had been included, the dance spread like a flame on Bonfire Night and everyone joined in:

With my rue-dum day, fol de riddle ray,
Wack fol de rol de riddle I-do!

* bleared – this means cried in Sussex dialect.
* glint – glimpse.
* glimmer-gowk – owl.
* daffy down dilly – daffodil.

5

Skylarks of Sussex

◎ The Ashdown Forest ◎

All, all that to the soul belongs,
Is closely mingled with old songs.

Eliza Cook, a poet who lived for a time on a small farm
in St Leonard's Forest near Horsham

After the Romans left Britain, the Saxons came to the South. They were a band of warrior pirates from Northern Europe, who arrived on the coast and like wolves among sheep, began to take over the land. The old name for South Saxons was 'Suthsaexe'. From 'Suthsaexe' came the name Sussex.

Words are as slippery as wet moss on the Ashdown Forest, that upside-down triangle of land that stretches seven miles up and seven miles across the top of this county.

The very name, Ashdown Forest, is slithery. Firstly, the Ashdown Forest is not a forest, it's a heath. A forest is dark, with tall trees growing close together, whereas a heath is wide open with low-growing plants like purple heather and yellow gorse. Secondly, you would think the word Ashdown comes from a combination of Ash tree and Downs, when it actually comes from the Anglo-Saxon name 'Aescadun', meaning Aesca's Dun. Aesca was a powerful fairy or sprite, and 'dun' meant hill.

We have slipped down a bank of words and landed with our feet firmly on the soil.

Ashdown Forest means 'the hill of Aesca'. The name Aesca was a mixture of sounds from nature: the 'eee, eee' of birds singing and the 'aaah, aaah' of animals panting. Not all Saxons were fighters, many were farmers and came with their families, who loved the land. The Saxons believed that they had to look after Sussex because it held the spirit of Aesca. The hills were her body and the stars were her eyes.

Aesca was forgotten until, not so long ago, a ranger on the Ashdown Forest lay in bed. He couldn't sleep. Was it the full moon? Was he overtired from cutting the scrubland? Had he stayed up too late writing his notes? If he didn't rest, how would he have the strength to work in the morning? He threw off his blanket.

His heart tapped at his chest like a woodpecker. 'You're lonely!' it seemed to say. 'You need a companion! When did you last sing, or dance?'

'I have no time to sing! I have no time to dance!' grumbled the ranger back to his own heart.

He shut his eyes and sighed, long and hard. When he opened them again, a woman was sitting beside him. She had brown hair, a cloak made of sacks and a simple, pale, cotton dress. 'You're never alone in the forest!' she whispered. 'I'm always here.' And, leaning towards him, she sang a fluting lullaby. She had only sung one verse before he fell asleep:

Just picture the bluebell and helleborine,
The purple bell heather and marsh moss so green,
Remember wood sorrel and hay-scented fern,
The bright golden gorse buds that make the
heath burn.

The next morning, as he went about his business, the ranger noticed the sun on the bracken and he didn't feel lonely. That night as he lay in bed he shut his eyes and began to run over the pictures of his day. As he was drifting off, he was aware of the woman singing, but he was asleep before she had finished the second verse:

Remember the fallow, the roe and red deer,
The shearing of sheep in the spring of the year,
Remember the cows and the full flowing milk,
And dragonfly lace upon lakes of soft silk.

The next night, the ranger was determined to stay awake. He kept his eyes wide open to see how she got into his room. Was it through the locked door or the window, open only a finger's breadth? He must have blinked because there she was again, singing. He was asleep by the time she'd finished the third verse:

Just think of the Blackcap, the Linnet and Lark,
The 'croak' of the Nightjar that 'creaks' through the dark,
Consider the Siskin 'chit chatter tea, tea!'
The quick Yellowhammer 'bread, bread, bread no cheese'.

The next night he waited and waited but she never came again.

One morning he decided to go and look for her. He packed himself a sandwich and started walking. He hadn't got very far when a fox started nibbling at the toe of his boot. 'You're hungry!' he said, and fed the fox some crumbs.

It ran ahead, looking behind as if encouraging the ranger to follow. Beside a stream, the fox shot into his sandy earth, but on the other side of the water were one hundred and fifty girls, some had gold hair, some red and some black. They were

dancing. The ranger began to wave and shout because there she was, the brown and white girl that had sung him a lullaby for three nights!

'Come to me, come!' he called.

'Not now!' she called back. 'Come to me next year – same time, same place. Now I'm a girl, then I'll be a bird. Pick me out from the others and I'll be yours!'

'What's your name?' he shouted.

'Aesca!' she replied.

He waited the full year. By day he seemed to hear her voice all over the heath: in the wind, the water, the hoof beats of deer, the rustling of shrews and the slithering of snakes. By night, his dreams were full of wings.

The next year he came to the banks of the stream and there were one hundred and fifty birds – pipits and redpolls, cuckoos and crossbills, firecrests and finches – so many! But, where was she? It was only when he saw a very ordinary little bird with brown and white feathers and a tiny crest that he began to blush and cry out.

'You! Aesca! It's me! I've found you. It's been a long year. Come to me, come!'

She cocked her head and kept her distance and only when he stopped speaking and stood very still did she come:

Peck peck hop, hop, peck peck hop hop.

'Keep on! Don't stop!' he said, willing her closer.

With a flutter and a flick, she perched beside him on the yellow gorse.

As slow as mist moving across the river, he raised his hands, but as he touched her, he felt his fingers begin to feather, his feet begin to claw and his body begin to shrink. He was becoming a small brown and white bird! He fluttered into the air uncertainly, but she was beside him, singing, as the other birds rose with them:

Let's swish with the Chiffchaff a 1,2,1,3,
Take off with the Stonechat, 'chack, chack, chack,
chack chee!'
Let's loop and let's sing and go soaring so free,
And swoop with the Kestrel a 'ki ki ki ki'.

So, if you are walking over the heathland of Ashdown Forest and see two skylarks circling around each other, it will be the ranger and Aesca, the birds that watch over Sussex.

6

Devil's Dyke

◎ Hove, Poynings ◎

Flour of England, fruit of Spain,
Met together in a shower of rain;
Put in a bag tied round with a string:
If you'll tell me this riddle, I'll give you a ring.

Traditional riddle (answer at the end of this story)

The Devil was hopping, stropping, smashing, crashing, lashing, flashing mad!

And his nose still hurt from his meeting with St Dunstan (see Story 2, 'The Devil and St Dunstan').

He felt like a fox in the weald; churches hemmed him in like hounds and he was unable to cavort until after dusk. With a butt of his horns he knocked off the nearest spire. Sparking the flint, he tore up brambles, spat blackberries and bounced from Seaford to Newhaven, Newhaven to Peacehaven and Peacehaven to Saltdean. He was just warming up.

As he boinged about Sussex like a parkour artist he heard snatches of songs from the children as they got ready for bed:

> *At Nutley Green the Devil was seen,*
> *At Wealden he was shod,*
> *At Mark's Cross he fell of his hoss,*
> *The Crawley Coven,*
> *Threw him in the oven.*
> *And ate him bones and all.*

He would give them something to sing about! But how? He sat on a blue shingle beach and a great grey wave slopped over him, battering him with pebbles. He wondered, 'Why did I ever love Sussex? Claggy* sea! Stubby cornfields!' He clenched his claws.

'**Boring!**' he yelled.

He had a point. In those days, Sussex was as flat as a pancake with a dusting of chalk like icing sugar.

Just for fun, when the first star appeared he ripped it out of the sky and threw it at Hove. It's still there, glittering in the park. The locals call it Golding Rock.

'Now that's more interesting!' said the Devil. It gave him an idea. 'I'll tear up Sussex and drown the lot of you!'

Nobody was listening. When the sun went to sleep, so did the people. Since the arrival of St Dunstan there had been no parties or dancing; there was no rollicking laughter after midnight. And as in those days there was no blue light interference from mobiles or tablets, the people slept like the dead.

'Which you soon will be!' guffawed the Devil.

Scratching the salt from his hairy shins and flicking the ticks off his furry head he shot into the air.

'I'll drown you all!' he bellowed.

He leaped to Poynings Village, where the trees and houses stood like inky blots against the night. Lowering his horns, he started to plough a channel through the soil. When his neck grew tired, he turned round, raised his shaggy behind and kicked with bucking hooves. He gouged flint, raised turf, pounded earth and piled up the land on either side. You can still see where his hooves and claws have scored the rocks.

His plan was to dig a trench all the way to the sea so it would sweep inland and swallow up Sussex. If he'd really wanted to do it, he wouldn't have paused for a single breath, a solitary fart or a solo burp until all of Sussex was underwater, until all its people were beneath the waves, with fishes floating in their empty skulls and seaweed twisting through their pearly bones.

If he had been less playful and kept his mind on the job, if he'd been more like, say, St Dunstan of Mayfield, he would have done it. He would have forged, not Devil's Dyke, which only took him five minutes, but Devil's Gorge, which would have taken him all night. It would have been hard work, but he could still have been safe underground by daybreak.

But the Devil found it impossible to concentrate. He leapt up high and landed on his hairy buttocks, so heavily the land tipped like a seesaw and made a slide.

'Wheeeee!'

He bounced and slid a thousand, thousand, thousand times; up, up and down, down, which is why the slopes of Sussex are called 'the Downs'. That done, he grabbed shoulder loads of earth and flung them in every direction to make hills and ridges.

To get a better view of his handiwork, he catapulted to the moon.

Grannie Annie was the only one awake. She was making Sussex Plum Pudding for her grandchildren, who were visiting the next day. With all the rumpus outside it was difficult to keep a steady hand weighing out suet and sugar.

'Probably the Devil. Best ignore him,' she grumbled. But when her house shook, she crossed herself, getting flour on her apron.

'Tut!' Brushing it off, she glanced up and saw the Devil's silhouette, horns and hooves against the moon. Where she had once had an unbroken view of the stars, stood hills. She heard gurgling. A river was running by her window where no river had been before.

Glancing at the clock she saw that there were still five hours before dawn. The rate the Devil was going, Sussex would be very untidy before sunrise. And that would never do.

Quick as you can crack an egg, she balanced a sieve on its side in the window, lit a candle and put it behind the sieve.

Without stopping to put on her slippers, she wet-footed it into the yard, where the

cockerel was sleeping on his perch, his head under his wing.

Grannie Annie stroked his purple and black feathers, ran a finger down his curly red crest, then shoved him off his perch.

'Cock a doodle doo!' scrabbled the bird in shock.

The Devil turned. He saw a glow in the east. Never considering for a moment that it might be a candle diffused by a sieve, he panicked: 'The sun is rising! I've been having as much fun as a Wessex Saddleback* in clover!' With a screech, he sprang towards the Channel.

The old woman carried on making her Sussex Plum Pudding, adding a few raisins by way of celebration.

The next morning the people of the county saw that their landscape was no longer flat. Instead, before them lay the ridges of the Downs, Ditchling Beacon, Rackham Hill, Mount Caburn and Chanctonbury Ring. The Sussex we know today.

As for the Devil, he hurdled across the sea, heading for a tin mine in Cornwall where he could hide from the light. A piece of earth fell from his hoof forming the Isle of Wight. Then he was gone.

But not for long.

* Wessex Saddleback – a breed of pig (see page 109)
* Claggy – dirty

Riddle answer: Plum Pudding.

7

Smuggler's Boots

◎ Isfield, Burling Gap ◎

Running round the woodlump
if you chance to find
Little barrels, roped and tarred,
all full of brandy-wine,
Don't you shout to come and look,
nor use 'em for your play.
Put the brishwood back again –
and they'll be gone next day!

Rudyard Kipling, 'A Smuggler's Song'. Kipling lived in
Sussex from 1897–1936

A long time ago when Sussex was the smuggling capital of England, there was a tiny farm south of Piltdown and north of Isfield, where the Ouse River wanders through the water meadows before turning south to hold hands with the River Uck.

A man lived at the farm with his four children. The youngest, Tom, was a boy of five, the second youngest, Don, a boy of six and a half, the middle child, Ron, a boy of eight and three-quarters and the eldest, Mary, a girl of fourteen and five-sixths.

Life was hard since their mother died giving birth to Tom. Each child pitched in: bird scaring, flint picking and sheep shearing, but of all of them, their father worked the hardest. He was up before sunrise and back just before tea after a day of digging, hoeing, fencing, ploughing, seeding or harvesting, according to the season.

At dusk, when their father finally came in through the low kitchen door, he would stand by the fire. Reaching up, now with this arm, now with that, he would arch and flex to stretch away the tension of the day:

'Ahhhhh!'

When he heard the satisfying crack of his aching back, he would sit down next to the hearth on his favourite chair, take off his boots and rub his feet together like a pair of snuggling ferrets. At the liberation of his wiggling toes, a broad, warm smile would cover his face. He was always very particular where he put the boots – not so close to the fire that they dried out too fast, nor so far away that they were still damp come morning. He'd had them sixteen years – they were a wedding present from his late wife and so well made that they would last a lifetime – they'd have to! With four young mouths to feed he would certainly never be able to afford another pair like them. Nevertheless, he knew that for as long as he and the children were fit, well, and able to work, they'd get by.

Despite his heavy workload he was always generous in giving time to others. Early one summer morning as the birds were singing in the dew, he was helping a neighbour build a barn by the Shortbridge road, when a weighty timber slipped its rope and fell on him. The other men carried him back to his little house and put him into bed. Mary mopped his brow and fed him chicken soup, but it was clear that the heavy beam had injured him inside very badly. His forehead grew hot with fever. Realising that he would not recover, he sent the boys about their chores and spoke to Mary alone.

'My girl, you make me very proud. You always work hard and take such care of your young brothers, I've no doubt you'll look after them when I am gone.'

'No, Father …' she tried to object, but he raised a shaky hand to silence her.

'Remember that nothing's worth more than family. Apart from that there are two things on this farm which are invaluable to you:

The first is our copper brood mare, Gladys. She's the envy of any man that sets eyes on her. The fine foals she bears and the work she does around the farm will make the difference between you having more than enough and going hungry. Take good care of her, set a guinea or two aside each time you sell one of her foals and eventually you'll have the money to replace her once she's old and out to pasture. Never sell Gladys. No man round here will offer what she's worth.

The second thing of value are my boots. They're the finest ever owned by anyone in our family. Since your feet are largish for a girl and mine are smallish for a man they might well fit you. Take good care of them and they'll take good care of you.'

Then he reached beneath the mattress and pulled out a purse. 'Here's all the money we have. It's not much but it will be enough to keep you going as long as you're careful.'

In a rasping whisper, he called for the boys and told each one how much they were loved and with that he breathed his last.

The girl and her brothers worked hard through the autumn and winter and survived. In the spring, the mare bore a foal, long-legged and full of life. They called her Copper because she was the same colour as her mother.

It wasn't long before Mary noticed that men were coming to lean on the fence of the paddock to view the splendid mare and foal. They stood at the edge of the field pointing and nodding. Mindful of their value, Mary began to keep them close to the house.

One night there was a storm. Lightning flashed, the wind wailed, the rain drummed and the rumble of thunder drowned out every other sound.

When Mary went to check on the horse and its foal in the morning, they were gone. She ran inside and shook Tom, Don and Ron awake. They searched every corner of Piltdown and Isfield without success.

For the next two weeks, Mary put on her father's boots and set off to look further and wider. But no one had news of Gladys and Copper.

Coming back from Hassocks one evening, she met Charlie, the wandering poet whose only home was the hollow of an old oak and the many lines of verse which filled his head. He bowed, saying, 'You've not lived till you've done something for someone who can never repay you.'

Mary understood he was asking for food or money. She gave him her last apple.

'Thank you, Mary. You're as kind and as generous as your father was. There's many a time I recite my lines to empty pockets. Nobody has anything for a poet in these days of thieves and smugglers.'

'It's a pleasure,' said Mary simply.

'Where have you been and where are you going?' asked the poet.

'I've been to Hassocks and now I'm going home,' she said. 'You'd be very welcome to share a meal with me and my brothers.'

Once inside the small house, Mary showed Charlie to her father's seat by the fire and invited him to sit. She removed her boots and placed them near the hearth, not so close as they dried too quickly, not so far as they'd stay damp. Charlie eyed them.

'As the Russian man said, "I prefer a good pair of boots to Shakespeare!" and those are fine indeed, but Hassocks and back? What you need is a horse!'

Mary's voice quivered as she told Charlie about the loss of Gladys and Copper.

'Everyone can master a grief but she that has it!' recited Charlie in a voice so kind Mary allowed herself all of two tears. He continued, 'I was at Birling Gap a few days ago and I saw a mare with a white blaze and a copper foal in a paddock by the inn.' He shrugged. 'I didn't stay long, mind – smugglers everywhere!' He tapped his nose and whispered, 'Watch the wall, my darling, as the gentlemen go by …'

After tea, and despite Mary's offer of shelter for the night, Charlie levered his bones out of the chair and shambled off into the dusk, blowing Mary a kiss as he tipped his threadbare top hat.

The next morning Mary packed some apples and her father's purse and strode out of the farm. Tom was sweeping the yard, Don was feeding the chickens and Ron was fixing a fencepost.

'Look after each other – I may be gone a few days!' she called over her shoulder.

Mary followed the river to Isfield, walked the gentle curves to Ringmer and traipsed the chalky tracks to Glynde, where she stopped to drink from a well and eat an apple before starting the slow climb towards Alfriston.

At dusk, she reached East Dean. Walking down the hill in the gathering darkness she heard the gulls and the waves slapping at Birling Gap. She saw an empty paddock next to the inn. As she entered, the smell of beer and sweat made her cough. Unshaven men, eyes hidden beneath their hats, huddled around their tankards at the tables. Their low voices fell away to silence as they noticed the girl's presence in the room.

A young woman with a flouncing dress laced up at the front clicked her scuffed boots and put her fists either side of her silver belt buckle. 'What do you want, farm girl?' she growled.

'Do you have a bed for the night?'

'How much have you got?'

'I can pay a shilling.'

'For a shilling, you'll have to share. The other lady snores.'

Mary nodded and followed the barmaid up the musty stairs until they reached a small room in the rafters.

'Will this suit your ladyship?' she sneered and then with a mocking drawl, 'Can I help with anything else?'

Mary couldn't resist, 'I don't suppose you've seen a copper mare with a foal?'

She gazed steadily at the barmaid whose cheek began to twitch.

'I wouldn't ask questions around here if you know what's good for you,' she flashed, flicking her head towards a rough straw mattress slung under the slope of the roof.

As she slammed the door behind her, a noise like the ungreased axle of a laden hay wagon filled the small space. Mary looked at the old lady snoring on the bed. As she breathed out, a moth dropped from a beam and flew across her face. She snored again, sucked it up into her nose, then coughed and breathed it out through her mouth. The moth flew as fast as it could towards the only candle in the room.

Mary heard voices outside and looked through the tiny window into the night. Men with burning torches were carrying wooden barrels out of the inn and into the stables. A small, restless man pointed and gestured with one hand and held up his torch with the other. Mary saw that his face was fine boned and foul tempered. The other men tensed as they passed near him; every so often he gave one of them a shove. With a sudden twist of his neck, he looked up towards the window and Mary drew back. Charlie's words made sense in an instant:

Watch the wall my darling as the gentlemen go by …

They were smugglers. And they had seen her see them.

She sat down on the edge of her hay mattress and took out the last of her apples, but was too anxious to eat. She decided to pretend to be asleep, just in case anyone came to check. She quickly untied the laces of her boots, placed them by the door and leaped into bed.

She was so tired her legs ached and she longed to comfort herself by rubbing one foot on top of the other, but she was too frightened to move. When she heard heavy steps on the stairs, her heart seemed to beat in her ears. The door burst open. Without opening her eyes, she knew it was the small man.

'What do you mean coming to my inn, asking questions and watching from windows?'

Mary opened bleary eyes. 'Sorry?' she said in a sleepy voice.

'Who are you?' the smuggler innkeeper demanded.

'I'm Mary – just a farm girl looking for my horse and her foal. I've been asking everywhere. She was lost in last month's storm.'

The man snorted. 'A farm girl who spies from windows?' At that moment, a gunshot echoed outside, then a loud, commanding voice boomed, 'The inn is surrounded. Surrender yourselves, we're coming in.'

It was Captain Crosby and his Customs Officers, looking for smuggled goods – contraband.

The small man strode towards Mary, face red, fist raised, but stopped sharply as he noticed the old lady's dress and bonnet on a chair. He grabbed them and pulled them on over his own clothes. As he made for the door, he saw Mary's boots and snatched them up.

'You can't have those, they were my father's!' Mary shouted.

He laughed at her. 'I've already taken your mare and foal – now I'll take your boots for your nosiness!' He laced them up swiftly and slipped through the door, locking it as he left.

Mary banged and shouted so loudly that the old lady turned on her side in her sleep.

Downstairs, the smuggler innkeeper rushed out through the main door, making his voice high like a woman's. This, combined with his small stature, fooled the Customs Officers into thinking he was an innocent female guest.

'Help, help! Did I hear the word smugglers? Let me out of here!' He fanned his face and made to faint. An officer caught him. 'Please, pity a young woman and escort me to the road.'

Deciding that a hysterical girl would hinder their search, the officer kindly escorted the very man they wanted outside.

The officers searched the inn from bottom to top, discovering secret passages and hiding holes, all empty. Eventually, they found Mary and the old woman in the rafters.

'Did you catch the horse thief?' Mary blurted to Captain Crosby.

'Who do you mean?' he replied. 'Apart from the serving staff, we've found only one young woman and set her on her way safely.'

When Mary explained that the innkeeper had taken the old woman's dress and stolen her father's boots, the Captain rushed back down the stairs. Mary followed. It was too late. The innkeeper/smuggler/horse thief was long gone. Crosby shook his head. 'It wouldn't have done any good anyway. We know this man is a smuggler and a thief, but we've never managed to find the proof. Even this search of the inn has been fruitless, which is a great shame. If you had been able to provide us with the evidence leading to his arrest you'd have received a £500 reward!'

Now Mary shook her head. 'It's not in the inn, it's in the stables. I saw them moving it all by torchlight.' She led the officers to the outbuilding. Once inside, she noticed that the straw in the middle of the floor was fresher than round the edges. She grabbed a broom from the wall and started to sweep, revealing a trapdoor. Beneath it a staircase led down into a secret cellar. The Customs Officers found it piled high with tubs of spirits, chests of tea and bales of silk, all contraband. While they searched the store, the girl heard the whinnying of a foal and the whickering of a mare. It was coming from the back of the stables.

'Gladys! Copper!' At the rear of the building, in the last stall, she found them and threw an arm round each of their necks.

The Customs Officers worked all night loading the illegal goods into an official wagon to be taken into safekeeping then auctioned off. Mary slept in the hay alongside her animals and in the morning rode Gladys homewards, leading Copper in a halter.

Meanwhile, in Falmer, Charlie was sitting on a fence beside the road. He took out the last of the apples Mary had given him. He was about to start munching his way through it, when he saw a tired looking young woman trudging towards him. Her dress was old and faded as was her bonnet. She looked as if she had walked through the night.

'My dear!' said Charlie. 'Please accept this! The apple falls when ripe!'

The young woman snatched it from his hand without a word of thanks and took a big bite.

A group of riders came around the corner. They were Customs Officers. Their leader greeted the pair.

'Good morning, Sir, good morning, Miss. Have either of you seen a smuggler disguised as a woman travelling this road?'

The poet shook his head. The young woman munched her apple.

'Just a pair of tramps,' muttered one of the officers. 'Let's go.'

But as they reined round their horses, Charlie saw something that made him leap to his feet. 'He's here! He's here! And he's wearing stolen boots!'

Charlie had only seen the rounded toes of the boots, but he would have recognised them anywhere. They were Mary's and had belonged to her father. The young woman tried to escape through a hedge, but Charlie was up so fast his top hat flew off. He caught the rascal by the apron strings as an officer put his gun in the small of his back.

'Where's Mary?' shouted the old poet. But the smuggling horse thief only spat.

It was Charlie who led the officers to the little farm south of Piltdown and north of Isfield, where Mary received her reward of £500. She used it to breed horses but she never sold Gladys or Copper. She and her brothers built Charlie a house with a desk and books and writing paper to last a lifetime. Although he spent many happy hours scratching away with his pen or sitting beside the fire, he was often on the road reciting his lines of poetry and tipping his threadbare top hat to the empty pockets of passers-by, but now it didn't matter; his pockets were full of apples and pennies. He considered himself very lucky and as he liked to say:

An ounce of luck is better than a pound of gold, but if gold comes your way then who's to complain?

8

A Sackful of Pig

◎ Beeding Hill, Steyning ◎

Fairy: Those that Hobgoblin call you, and
sweet Puck,
You do their work, and they shall have
good luck.
Are not you he?
Puck: Thou speakest aright:
I am that merry wanderer of the night.

Shakespeare: A Midsummer Night's Dream

It's me again, Puck, to rhyme with luck and muck. I love horses: carthorses, racehorses, horseradish. My little brother Flick – that's Flick to rhyme with quick and trick – loves them even more than me. He's always whispering in their ear to tell them where to find marigolds or to warn them rain is coming.

Human beings don't understand us. They call us fairies. They think we live in the bells of bluebells or the gloves of foxgloves. We don't live anywhere! We're as free as the wind or a wave on the sea. They think because we're

small we must have small brains. They talk to us like we're babies, all 'coochie coo' or 'iddy bid'. I speak every language of this world. I can zip to Zanzibar in a second, to Bora Bora in a blink, but I happen to like Sussex so quite often I'm here. But don't count on me. I can't say when I'll appear and I can't say why – I just like to fly.

One thing I do know: I prefer animals to humans and horses to cars.

Back in the days when carthorses set the speed of life, I had some good friends: Violet, Jim, Lion and Traveller. They would plod along the lanes, jingling their harnesses and dipping their great heads to munch at snapdragons. They worked all day pulling heavy carts full of beer barrels or hay bales or anything that would make their owners money. They belonged to two carters who couldn't sing a song between them. They didn't feed the horses enough either and for that we blew wheat-dust up their noses to make them sneeze and kicked their hair to make it itch.

We secretly looked after the horses. We gathered them the sweetest hay, pale green or light gold, and threw away the rumpty stuff the carters gave them. We fetched the purest rainwater, carrying it in walnut shells and tipping it into their buckets. Our big friends grew strong and so shiny we could slide down their necks and dance upon their broad backs.

One midnight, we were working, polishing dust off the hay and carrying water, when one of the carters came in. Generally, we Little Folk rinse ourselves with black hellebore root and sunflower juice to be invisible to humans, but since the carters usually snored heavily till sunrise, we'd got slack. One of them threw open the door and slapped his sides with laughter.

'Oochie, coochie, if it isn't a little fairy wairy! Shall I fetch an incy, wincy, iddy, biddy saucer of milk?'

That was just too much blish-blash.* Flick and I were off and away. We flitted to India to feed watermelons to elephant calves.

A year had passed by the time we returned and we went straight to find Violet, Jim, Lion and Traveller. They were trying to graze in a dry ditch, so thin you could see their ribs. We were gathering hay and rainwater when we caught sight of the carters on Beeding Hill. They were finishing off a rabbit they had roasted over the fire and discussing their misfortune.

'We've been poor ever since those horses grew so thin they couldn't pull a hand-cart. What we need is a prize-winning pig to sell in exchange for a fat purse.'

'You wouldn't be thinking of that fine Wessex Saddleback sow they've just inherited at old Dip Farm?'

'I am. Let's steal her tonight and take her to Thakeham Fair tomorrow.'

'While we're at it, we can sell those useless horses for dog meat. Ow! Dratted midges.'

They slapped their own heads and faces as Flick pinched their ears and I pulled their hair. We were kicking, spitting cross, but we stayed with the carters as they walked through the woods, across the track and into

Dip Farm. The barns had holes in the roofs and the paint of the farmhouse was peeling. The carters crept into the pigpen with the biggest, strongest sack they could find and a satchel full of acorns. Carefully they hitched open the gate and laid a trail of acorns out into the yard. The pig came quietly, scooping up each little snack with a grunty, sniffly whiffle. She followed the thieves away from the barns, across the track, through the woods to the bottom of Beeding Hill.

It had worked a treat; the two carters began to punch each other with delight. They grabbed the sow and squeezed her into the sack, then heaved her, squealing, onto their shoulders and set off.

She was big and she was heavy and the men weren't halfway up the hill before they were puffing and sweating. They dropped the sack on the ground beside a big rock.

While they were bent double, catching their breath, I untied the mouth of the sack and let the pig out, ushering her behind the rock, as Flick leaped in to take her place, muttering:

Flick be as big as a saddleback,
Heavy as lead in the carter's sack.

The carter and his brother hoisted their load again and began to stagger up the slope.

I ran along behind. After a few feet I shouted out, 'Flick, Flick, where are you?'

Flick answered loud and clear in his shrill voice:

In a sack,
Pick-a-back,*
Riding up Beeding Hill.

'A talking pig!' screamed the carters. They dropped the sack. One circled left, the other circled right until they crashed into each other, fell over, and rolled down the hill into a big pile of horse manure.

Flick climbed out of the sack saying, 'Humans are all the same! I bet you a penny the old couple who own Dip Farm are no better than those carters.'

I can never resist a wager so I replied, 'I bet you a sixpence they are!'

At daybreak, we herded the sow back to the farm along with the horses to test the old couple. The farmer was sitting on the step having a quiet moment before he started his day. Flick leaped onto the end of his pipe, gave a bow, then jumped down onto the ground, waiting for his reaction. The farmer merely nodded and carried on looking at the horizon. I tried a little jig in the dust of the yard but all he said was 'Morning,' from the corner of his mouth. Then he tapped his pipe on the door frame and ambled over to the animals. The farmer's wife hobbled out of the kitchen with a bucket of leftovers for the pig. When she caught sight of us she simply smiled and said, 'Nice to see you, Good Folk,' then crossed the yard to the sow. 'G'wan Ivy,' she huffed gently and the pig waddled back to her pen.

The farmer patted the necks of Violet, Jim, Lion and Traveller. 'You four look like you could do with some proper rest and good feed.' As he led them into the stable, he began to sing gruffly:

I am a brisk and bonny lad and free from care and strife,
And sweetly as the hours pass I love a country life,
At Thakeham Fair I'm often there, midst pleasure to be seen,
Though poor, I am contented and as happy as a Queen.

It was true: apart from the sow, the couple were very poor, but still the horses were each given a net of the sweetest hay and a bucket of well water.

I turned to Flick, surprised but gleeful at winning my bet:

Sixpence lost, sixpence lost,
Who'd have guessed that kindness costs!

It wasn't long before our horse friends were gleaming and strong once more and with our help, Dip Farm prospered. Ivy had litter after litter of squealing piglets and Violet, Jim, Lion and Traveller helped the farmer plough the fields. When the harvest was brought in, the new barns were filled from stone floor to wooden roof.

And in the time of harvest, how cheerfully we go,
Some with hooks and some with crooks and
some with scythes to mow.
And when our corn is free from harm we have
not far to roam,
We'll all away to celebrate the welcome
Harvest Home.

'Brisk and Bonny Lad', from the Copper
Family Songbook

* blish-blash – idle talk.
* pick-a-back – to carry.

9

The Lychpole Highwayman

◎ Lychpole ◎

No I ain't seen Turpin pass this way,
Neither do I want to see him this long day,
For he robbed my wife all of ten pounds,
A silver snuffbox and a new gown,
For I'm the hero, the Turpin hero,
I am the great Dick Turpin ho.

Jim Copper remembered this song being sung by Fred
'Nobby' Earle, a farm labourer of Rottingdean

To go from Lancing to Steyning, you take the A27 and the A283, but a few hundred years ago the only road was cut into the grass and chalk of the Downs. Today we journey by car, but back then the main way to travel was on horseback, in a carriage, or on foot.

At night, this lonely road was preyed upon by a highwayman so pitiless it was said his heart was as hard as downland flint, and that's how he came be known as Flint.

He was rich. By day, a gentleman in silk breeches and a waistcoat with silver buttons; by night, a robber with tricorn hat, eye mask and cloak the colour of darkness. His horse, Nero, was also black.

A lord and lady with their children, covered in furs and half asleep, might start awake as they heard the coachman's cry and felt the carriage horses pull up sharply on the lonely road. Looking through the window they would see Nero pawing at the grass with a foreleg, Flint astride him, brandishing his pistol that fired bullets of lead. Flint's voice

was like a millstone grinding grain as he flung open the carriage door:

Lead for you, or gold for me?
Speak now, sharpish, what'll it be?

All inside would deliver whatever he demanded, choosing to give up their riches and keep their lives.

Then Flint was off. He knew the Downs like his own skin and loved them like a mother. He leaned close into Nero's neck, galloping fast as a gunshot through the gorse.

Time after time, they eluded the king's officers who were always only a few heartbeats behind, combing the roads. As they passed within feet of him, hidden in the folds of a ridge or concealed by a stand of windblown trees, Flint clutched his ribs with one hand and beat the air with the other, his mouth wide open with silent laughter.

Being hated by the whole of Sussex made Flint's eyes glitter and gave him the edge he needed to run the nightly race he always won. The frightened pleas of those he robbed thrilled him. It was a pleasure to hear from a great lady that the ring he ripped from her was a gift from her grandmother. It delighted him to learn that the watch he wrestled from a lord had cost a hundred guineas. He chuckled that the coins he snatched from children were their carefully saved pennies.

Flint enjoyed being a celebrity, but it couldn't last forever.

One wet night, he rode Nero off a bank down into the road in front of a carriage. The driver was so startled that he braked too hard, tipping the coach on to its side and blocking the road. The wheels were still spinning in the air when Flint heard shouting and pounding hooves behind him. The King's Officers were closing in. He urged Nero forward to get around the stricken carriage, but the verge was peppered with shards. The horse trod his forefoot on a stone and shied. Flint kicked him on, but could tell from the uneven rhythm of Nero's stride and his dropped shoulder that he was lame. He jumped to the ground and ran towards a gully, riding boots slithering on the damp grass, but the mounted King's Officers were faster.

The highwayman fell heavily. His swag bag flew up into the air. When the officers retrieved it from the mud they found a silver teaspoon for a christening, gold teeth and the jewelled dagger used to extract them, necklaces, coins, earrings and all manner of jewellery taken at pistol point from the rich, the poor, the deserving and, more often than not, the undeserving.

Hands bound, Flint was led through the cold rain to the gallows tree by Lychpole farm. As the guards marched him forward, he ducked low, loosening their grip on his shoulders. He kicked the legs out from under the man on his left, barged the man on his right into a ditch and ran until he heard the unmistakable click of a pistol being cocked behind him. He turned. Smirking, the Captain sat high on his horse looking down at Flint, gun aimed at his head:

Lead for you, or hanging tree?
Speak now, sharpish, what'll it be?

Although he knew what awaited him, Flint smirked back. 'You think you're the law in this place?' He shook his head. 'You can take my horse, you can take my life, but there is an older, greater power than you in these Downs,' he turned his face up towards the sky. The rain ran off his ears and chin as he shouted at the rumbling thunder: 'Prince of Darkness! Hear me! I offer you my soul! In return, let me be a highwayman forever!'

Only Flint heard the Devil's voice. It thrummed, like a hornet in his head. 'I will take your soul! For as long as you are hated, you may terrorise these roads. But should anyone ever show you love, our bargain will be broken.'

When Flint was hanged, dazzling lightning set fire to the gallows tree before the rain put it out with a hiss. Flint's body was buried without a prayer, face down in the road, his head pointing west. When the sun rose, there was a pile of earth and the grave was empty.

That night, a priest was riding home, thinking about the wine he would have on reaching his armchair. His pony reared. In the middle of the road, a man with eyes glowing beneath his tricorn hat rasped:

Lead for you, or gold for me?
Speak now, sharpish, what'll it be?

When the priest came to, in the dew he found his purse was empty.

There's only one thing worse than a highwayman and that's a phantom highwayman. The ghost of Flint held up men, women, children, the elderly, the rich, the poor and everyone in between. Many fainted, others emptied pockets as they ran. One evening, rather than give up his passengers, a coachman galloped his carriage at Flint and passed right through him! Spooked, the horses ran off the road, dragging the coach over the lip of a hollow. The travellers were scattered all over the ground like salt from a shaker. After that, no one travelled the road again at night.

In Steyning, a girl called Cara had been caring for her sick mother for weeks. Her father was away, fighting for Queen Anne in the Americas, and the girl was her mother's only help. The doctor told her to ease the fever by making a tonic of the yarrow plant which grew outside the town. Over the long period of her mother's illness, Cara had to go further and further afield to find the plant. She returned later and later and her mother grew more and more angry at having to wait for her medicine.

'Look at the time! Is it fun playing hopscotch while your mother suffers?' Cara let the complaints wash off her. She knew her mother was in pain.

Eventually, her search for yarrow took Cara so far away that she found herself walking home after dusk. Two small flames were coming towards her. She wondered what they might be. Was it a gentleman smoking two pipes at once? No, it was a pair of red eyes beneath the tricorn hat of a man with a gun.

Curious, Cara stared at the highwayman with her big brown eyes. She wasn't the kind of girl to get scared:

Lead for you, or gold for me?
Speak now, sharpish, what'll it be?

'I beg your pardon?' she said.

'Give me everything!' Flint's voice was harsh.

'All I have is this one penny, and I can't give it to you because I need it to buy bread and milk so that my mother and I can eat this week.' Cara held up a grubby coin in her palm. It vanished from her hand and Flint laughed as he walked away.

'What would a phantom highwayman want with one penny?' Cara called out.

Flint stopped and turned. 'What?'

Cara continued in a kind and steady voice: 'You must be very unhappy to be so mean and angry.'

'Are you mad? I love being a highwayman, always have and always will. I was mean when I was alive, and I'm meaner still dead.'

Cara looked doubtful.

'I'm evil! Run!' bellowed Flint.

Cara stood her ground. 'How did you come to be evil?' she asked. 'Did you love someone who died? Did you suffer in a war? I know that pain makes my mother very angry.'

'Turn your eyes away from me!'

Obediently Cara turned away, sighing, 'I'm so sorry for you.'

'I don't need pity,' Flint roared. 'I'm famous! I answer only to the Prince of Darkness!' He hoped that mentioning the Devil would turn Cara against him. It had the opposite effect.

'I'll pray for you. Take my money. If I had gold, I'd give the Devil every penny to free you, but all I've got is love!'

At the word 'love', lightning forked. Cara looked up at the sky and saw a shooting star. When she looked back, Flint had gone. In his place was a glittering pile of stolen treasure. Cara put it in her basket with the yarrow she had collected and went home to her mother.

First thing in the morning, she took the stolen valuables to the courthouse to be restored to those whom Flint had robbed, but since so much of it belonged to people long gone and untraceable, only a fraction of it could be returned. The rest the judge awarded to Cara.

She used it to buy better medicines and food for her mother, who grew from strength to strength and was fully well again within a few short weeks. She never shouted at her daughter again.

After that, Cara would often wander out onto the Lancing road at dusk, and leave white and yellow yarrow flowers by the carriageway, just so that Flint, wherever he was, would know he was always in her prayers.

10

The Shepherd and the Moon

◎ Saltdean, Telscombe ◎

Old Mother Slipper Slopper jumped out of bed,
And out of the window she poked her head,
Oh John, John, the grey goose has gone,
And the fox is off to his Den-o!

Folk song

There was once a shepherd boy called Pup
Moppet who was slow moving, slow speaking
and as clever as a magpie. He was long and
lanky and wore a cloak, buttoned-up leather
leggings and a billycock hat. His hands were
the colour of potatoes, so large he could fit
a full-grown hare in each palm. But despite
the thickness of his fingers, all the tunes Pup
played on his rusty mouth organ were sharp
and fast.

With his sheep, up there on the hills above
the sea, Pup felt like a sailor. He could taste
the salt on his lips and read the signs. Shoals
of porpoises heading east meant wind from
the west. If Worthing was visible, eighteen
miles down the coast, rain was coming.

It was February and Pup had been busy. He
had built the high-walled pens for the ewes
to protect them from the vicious north-east
winds, bedded them down in clean straw
and now he was feeding warm milk to an
orphan hob-lamb from the crooked stove of
his shepherd's caravan that he liked to call
his Den-o.

Outside, the frost was silently covering the stubby gorse and winter blackthorn. The moon was full and Pup was alert. One rustle from 'Maas Reynolds', Mr Fox, and he might find all his lambs savaged. He heard an owl. Sound travels a good distance on still nights and he guessed the bird was beyond Telscombe. A few moments later, he heard boots thudding over the turf. As the thuds got closer, Pup detected heavy wheezing and the sound of slopping inside wooden containers. He concluded two men were running away from something, each carrying a barrel full of whisky.

The fire in his stove had burnt low, which was lucky. Smugglers don't like to be seen. Pup bit his cheek, his ears prickled. He listened until the men were half a mile across the fields and when they were at the outermost edges of his hearing, he caught the faintest of splashes. Only then did Pup's face relax into a sly smile.

He left it an hour or two, took his shepherd's staff made of hazel wood, and set out across the white chalk paths towards the dew pond. The sides of his tongue tingled at the thought of whisky heating up his belly.

He came to the dew pond where he was sure the smugglers had thrown the barrels. The full moon shone on the water like a giant silver sovereign. Pup lay down on the crispy grass and, plunging his staff in the water, began to dredge the pond, forwards and backwards, searching for the whisky. For once, his concentration obliterated all sounds. He had just hit something when a voice so surprised him, he nearly tumbled in, head first.

'Who are you and where are you from?'

Pup was on his feet. A Customs Officer in white trousers, black top hat and blue jacket was standing on the other side of the pond. His smart gold buttons glittered in the moonlight.

Quick as a farmer drinks his first cider after loading the final bale at harvest, Pup had an idea. Speaking as slowly as a carthorse plods, he replied, 'I'm just a poor shepherd from the Village of Porridge!' He knew that shepherds had a reputation for being stupid and he played up to it, twisting his mouth to the side and twisting his cloak with his thick fingers.

'Where's that?' asked the Customs Officer, cracking his knuckles with irritation.

'It's a pinch of salt across from the Mine of Treacle.'

'Don't be an idiot! What are you doing?'

Pup widened his eyes then furrowed his brow, 'What am I doing? What am I not doing! Such a long day! It all started this morning when I put my boots on backwards. I didn't know if I was coming or going. Then the willow started weeping so I had to tie all my hankies on her branches. And when I finally got to my fields, I found they were sopping wet so I had to hang them out to dry. Why, that took till it was dark and now, because I've run out of candles, I'm fishing for the moon. When I hook her, I'll have a lamp for my room. I'm no gom'uril.'*

Pup whacked the pool and began to heave his staff out of the water: 'I think I've got her!

I think she's coming!' He groaned and pulled and splashed.

The Customs Officer was soaked. He flicked the tails of his jacket, brushed the dirty drips off his crisp trousers and strode away, muttering, 'Beetle head!'*

As soon as he was out of sight, quick as 'Maas Reynolds' himself, Pup hooked his crook, hauled up two barrels and took them back to his Den-o.

The following evening, long after the exhausted sun had flopped behind the line of the sea, Pup opened his first barrel of whisky. He gave each of his sheep some milk mixed

with a drop of the hot stuff, poured the tiniest dram for himself, picked up his mouth organ and began to play. When his stomach was as warm as a lamb nestled in the wool of its mother, Pup covered himself with a corn sack and, using a pile of grain for a pillow, fell asleep for a full hour.

I heard that those barrels of whisky kept Pup and his sheep warm for many winters.

---

* gom-uril – Sussex dialect meaning a silly person who talks too much.

* beetle head – daft person.

11

A Thimbleful of Sugar

◎ Rottingdean ◎

For there's many a dark and cloudy morning
Turns out to be a sun-shiny day.

Folk song: 'Banks of the Sweet Primroses'

Bob Copper was a man who loved to sing. His family had worked the land and fished the sea in the village of Rottingdean for 400 years. But during the Second World War, Bob became a police constable and one of his jobs was to investigate sudden deaths: bombing raids, planes falling into the sea, or just the kind of deaths that happen every day. It was a hard job for a young man.

One dark and cloudy morning he was called to West Street. A ten-month-old baby had died two days before and his very young mother wouldn't let go of him. She was all alone. The father of the baby was a Canadian squaddie – a soldier who had been posted abroad.

Bob knocked at the door. It was opened by a girl with red eyes and hair that was as matted as a cotted fleece.* 'Go away!' She turned her back, but left the door ajar. In her arms was her child, wrapped in rags and woollen blankets. She clutched him tightly. He still felt warm.

'He's still alive!' she shouted.

Bob didn't know what to do, and was relieved to hear the voice of old Mrs Tuppin behind him. She was famous for her home remedies and cooking and knew everything that was going on in the village. 'I think everybody needs a cup of tea!' she said briskly. Glad to have something to do, Bob lit the single gas ring, made tea and poured it into chipped enamel cups. He and Mrs Tuppin sipped in silence. The young mother glared at them for a while, then relaxed, sat down on the stained settee and began to rock the baby.

After a few minutes, Mrs Tuppin blinked her quick brown eyes, 'There now! I don't know why I didn't think of it before! I have a special recipe that will help the little one! All I need, my girl, is for you to fill this thimble with sugar from any house that lies between the hills and the sea and bring it back to me.'

Mrs Tuppin took out a little silver thimble engraved with leaves and flowers from her apron pocket. She used it every day to help her push her needle through thick cloth. 'Take it!' she said, hobbling over to the settee.

The young mother's eyes began to shine. 'Every house in Rottingdean is between the hills and the sea, someone will surely give me some sugar!'

Mrs Tuppin put a moth-eaten shawl around the girl's shoulders, but just as she was leaving, the old woman said, 'One other thing. The sugar must come from a house where the people have not felt the pain of death.'

The young mother nodded and ran out of the door, still clutching the child. She knocked at the first house a little anxious, because this was the war and sugar was rationed to eight ounces per person.

'Please may I have a thimbleful of sugar for my child?'

'Of course,' said the neighbour with one look at her and the bundle in her arms. 'You can have all our sugar for the week!'

'Just to check,' said the young mother, 'I need sugar from a house that hasn't felt the pain of death.'

A little girl appeared between the neighbour's knees.

'Purrkins my cat died last week,' she said, screwing up her face. 'I cried a lot.'

The young mother tried the next house, but it was a grandfather who had passed away. Every family in Rottingdean had suffered loss.

After a long morning of knocking on doors, the young mother turned back towards West Street where the old lady and Police Constable Bob were still waiting. Without a word, she handed the baby over to Mrs Tuppin, who said a prayer before reaching a second time into her apron to bring out a little pair of scissors. Taking a snip of the baby's soft hair, she put it into the silver thimble.

'Keep that to remember him by,' she said, and pressed it into the young mother's empty hand.

That evening as Bob Copper sang 'Banks of the Sweet Primroses' with his father and brothers round the fire, he came to the lines:

There is many a dark and a cloudy morning
Turns out to be a sun-shiny day.

He thought of the young mother in West Street and heartily wished her some sun.

And in years to come she managed to live with her sadness. She had many children, but she always kept the silver thimble on the mantelpiece and often stroked the whorl of silky hair within it.

* cotted fleece – a fleece matted together during growth.

12

The Rise of the Sussex Doughman

◎ Lewes, Alfriston and Firle ◎

I had a little hen, the prettiest ever seen,
She washed me the dishes and kept the house clean;
She went to the mill to fetch me some flour,
She brought it home in less than an hour;
She baked me my bread, she brewed me my ale,
She sat by the fire and told many a fine tale.

Traditional poem

The capital of Sussex is Lewes. Lewes is an ancient town which straddles the River Ouse and climbs up the High Street toward its very own castle. In days gone by, it was an important river port with a mint that made gold coins.

One frosty morning, a woman with silvery hair and a dress frayed at the cuffs and hem came to the town looking for kindness. She sat on the bridge over the river, took off her moth-eaten hat and held it out to passers-by. She was uncomfortable because the cobbles poked her thighs. The merchants walking by looked the other way or were too busy to notice her as they counted their gold coins, passing them from one hand to the other. At the end of the day, all she had succeeded in gaining was a hat full of peas someone had given her from their garden. This was not at all what she expected, but at least she'd have some supper.

Towards dusk, a large man with rosy cheeks walked past. 'Sir?' she said. He looked round. 'Over here, Sir.'

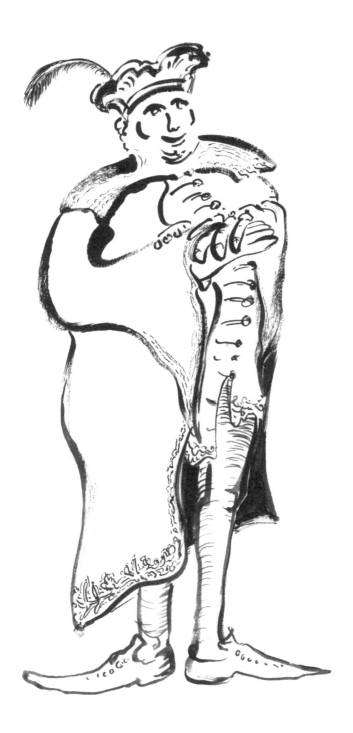

Leonard Lardycake looked down, saw her and screwed up his face. 'What do you want?' he asked.

She took in his long pointy shoes of soft leather, bright yellow stockings of fine wool, and embroidered jacket with sleeves to the ground. His velvet hat, the shape of a pie, was decorated with a feather.

'I'm hungry and cold – might I share one tiny corner of your good fortune?'

The man tutted and turned his back on the old woman.

'Sir?' the old woman called again.

'What is it now?' the man snapped.

'Begging your pardon, but what's your business?'

Now this posed a problem for Lardycake: on the one hand, he wanted to ignore the woman; on the other, he was not only the Mayor of Lewes, but also the most successful and prosperous baker in the town and therefore in all of Sussex. He could not bear to miss the opportunity to boast, even to an old woman in rags.

He turned to face her. 'I am the master baker of Lewes, I own nearly all the bakeries in this town. The men and women I employ sweat into the night to make the bread that feeds both great and humble. Not only that,' he broadened his shoulders, 'but take note, I am also the Mayor!'

'Certainly, Sir, I will take note. You are the Mayor, a man who has almost everything.'

'Almost? Almost? What do you mean almost? I *do* have everything!'

The old woman nodded. 'Yes, Sir, of course, Sir. Very nearly.'

'Very nearly?'

'Yes, Sir. Only one tiny thing missing.'

'What? What?'

'Everlasting fame. I could make you the most famous Mayor that ever was or ever will be.'

'How?' The baker's eyes bulged like a fish on the end of her line.

'All it would take is a tiny piece of gold.'

The baker hated giving anything to anybody, but could not resist the promise of everlasting fame, so with a sly smile he took a fat gold coin out of his purse and a pocketknife out of his pocket. 'A tiny piece of gold you say?' The woman nodded. He shaved a minuscule filing off the edge of the coin and dropped it into her hand. She had to squint to see it.

'There you are,' the Mayor said, 'our bargain is struck,' and as he walked off, he was laughing so much he trumped.

The woman was on her feet, surprisingly tall. 'Our bargain is struck indeed. I'll make you famous alright!' She picked up the frayed hems of her dress with such force they knocked over her hat full of peas. She crumpled.

Passing by at that moment, leading a scrawny old ram, was a boy. Quickly tying up the creature, the lad zipped here and there to rescue the peas.

'Don't worry! I'll get 'em, every one,' he shouted cheerfully and it wasn't long before they were all safe in the old woman's hat. He handed them back with a bow. 'Chols, at your service!'

His worn coat and jaunty cap made the old woman smile.

'I've just spent hours shelling those peas for my tea, thank you. I'm too old and stiff to go running and bending. You are very kind, young man, and one good turn deserves another. That is the scrawniest looking ram I've ever seen, where are you taking him?'

Chols looked sad and shook his head. 'He used to be big and strong, but he's been ailing recently with Dad being sick. Mum and I don't think there's any hope for him. He's a tough old beast but I'm taking him to the butcher.'

'No need for that,' the old woman said. 'Today's Midwinter. Take him to graze on the fat grass in the fairy ring at midnight tonight and he'll be good as new. Better, even.'

'Where is it?' Chols asked.

'Over by Burlough Castle in Alfriston,' she replied.

Chols swallowed. Alfriston was nine miles from Lewes over the Downs, and he'd have to climb Firle Beacon. It would take ages. Nevertheless, he thanked the woman and set off in the direction of Mount Caburn – what had he got to lose?

She called after him, 'Kindness always brings good luck!'

He turned to wave, but she had disappeared.

As night fell, Chols trudged along the eastern banks of the River Ouse, up flint paths, then leant against the cold wind from the sea as he topped Firle Beacon. After four hours he arrived at the mounds of Burlough Castle. The Downs stretched ahead for miles in the moonlight. The ground was cracked from being dried year-round by the constant gusts, but in a circle, several paces across, the grass was vivid green. Chols realised that this must be the fairy ring the old woman had described. He let the ram loose to graze. That done, he sat with his back against a wind-blown tree, tugged his coat close, pulled his hat over his eyes, and settled down for a chilly nap.

Back in Lewes, in all the Mayor's bakeries, men and women toiled, kneading and shaping dough into loaves, rolls, buns and baps and putting them into hot ovens. At midnight when the only other beings awake in the town were cats, rats and the odd duck on the river, the bakers in each of the Mayor's premises went to check their bread.

Mary in Sun Street opened the oven door and fainted. Egbert in Ferrers Road dropped his paddle (a spatula for lifting bread in and out of the heat). Alfred in St Peter's Place ran into the street screaming. At the same time, bakers from Southover High Street to Castle Keep were shocked and horrified by what they found in their ovens – or rather what they didn't find: each oven was cold and empty. All except one.

On St Nicholas' Lane, Will watched as the oven door opened and an enormous hand burst out of the flames. The hand became an arm, the arm became a shoulder, the shoulder became a whole body. A bread giant emerged, straightened his long legs, and crashed his head through the ceiling. He was twice the height of a tall man. Will stood in the doorway trembling, while the giant toasted himself in front of the oven door. As he turned from off-white to golden brown, Will snatched up his paddle. When the Doughman's hands and feet were dark and hard as hammers he took a step towards the door. Will tried to beat him back, but his paddle snapped on the hard crust. Will fled down the street.

Smashing his way out of the bakery, the bread giant sniffed the air and stomped off towards the High Street. He was making for the dairy on Cockshut Road. On finding it closed up, he roared, then kicked out, splintering the gates and sending the locks flying.

Once inside, the Doughman found the butter churns and started to eat and eat and eat and eat. By this stage, Will had woken the Constable, and all the bakers who had discovered their ovens empty, formed a mob. Brandishing torches, their angry clogs clattering on the cobbles of the streets, they pursued the bread giant, following its flakey trail to the dairy, which they found ruined and empty of butter. Every last churn had been licked clean then hurled aside, but the culprit himself was gone.

Awoken by the clamour, the terrified townsfolk peered out from behind their curtains. A pale old man in a nightcap threw open his window and pointed, 'That way! It went that way!'

The Doughman was striding up Lewes High Street. The mob pursued it, but it stopped and roared back at them.

One man had grabbed an ancient spear from above the fireplace on his way out of the White Hart Inn. He threw it now but it bounced off. Another shot an arrow into

the giant's bready belly – it went in through
the front and out through the back. The mob
fell silent. The Doughman shook his toasted
fists at them, then turned and ran faster
than a galloping horse in the direction of
Kingston. They had no hope of keeping up
as he disappeared into the copses and valleys
of the Downs.

Meanwhile, nine miles away over by Burlough Castle, Chols was nicely settled into his nap when a high-pitched noise woke him up. He held his breath and listened. Hearing the squeak again, Chols jumped to his feet and followed the sound to a crack in the middle of the fairy ring.

'Down here!' a tiny voice shouted.

He lay on the grass and saw a hand the size of a thumbnail waving from beneath the ground. 'A fairy!' He laughed to himself with delight, but not out loud of course, since he knew, as all Sussex people do, that to laugh at 'the pharisees'* – the fairies – brings very bad luck.

'Help! Help!' the voice cried.

'What's wrong?' Chols asked.

The fairy said:

My spatula, my wooden peel
Got broken as I baked my meal
Now bread will stick and cakes congeal!

I have no tools, I have no glue
Unless you mend and make it new
I don't know what on earth I'll do!

'Don't know what *under* the earth, more like,' Chols thought, but he was very handy, especially with his pocketknife, so he offered to have a go at fixing it. The wee arm passed the peel up – it was no bigger than a blade of grass, hardly enough to lift one biscuit.

Chols took it, and for nearly an hour in the moonlight he whittled with his pocketknife, shaping the break in the handle into a joint. Then he took a pin from the lapel of his coat and used that for a nail, repairing the peel so you'd never know it was broken. He handed it down through the crack in the ground. The fairy sang for joy:

> *That's one for me, now one for you,*
> *Come let me do a favour too.*

> *Seek out the stream that runs ahead,*
> *Like melting butter on warm bread.*

Then float a cart upon the road,
A frying pan within your load.

Not spiders, only flapping webs,
Will help you as the darkness ebbs.

Goodbye, good Chols!

Chols knew that fairies sometimes spoke in riddles but this seemed to him nothing but nonsense. He was about to ask what it all meant when the crack in the earth closed.

'Beheheh!'

Chols looked up – the ram's eyes were gleaming and he was as hefty as an ox after only a few hours of grazing. He was so strong, Chols was able to ride him all the way back to Lewes.

The clock was striking three in the morning when the boy came to the River Ouse.

'That's it!' he cried. '"The stream that runs ahead like melting butter on warm bread" is the River Ouse, or rather Ooooooze!'

He saw a rowing boat tethered to the bank. "'Float a cart upon the road" – the road must be the river and the cart must be a boat!'

He heard a quacking in the rushes. 'Ducks! Their feet are the "flapping webs" the fairy was talking about! So, according to the fairy, I must float this boat on the River Ouse. But why do I need a frying pan?'

As they climbed School Hill, Chols saw broken buildings and people running with burning torches. Something really bad must have happened while he was over by Alfriston. He bumped into the Constable.

'What's wrong?' he asked.

'The town is cursed,' came the reply. 'A bread giant rose from one of the Mayor's ovens. First he ransacked the bakery, then, smelling the butter in Cockshut Dairy, broke in to feed.'

'A giant bread man that loves butter!' mused Chols. 'Where is he now?'

'We've searched high and low, out towards Kingston and Rodmell, Barcombe and Plumpton. No sign. Who knows where he is and what he's up to! But as sure as butter's butter, he'll be back.'

'What has the Mayor done about it?'

'What Mayor? The greedy baker was last seen heading out on the Offham Road with a sackful of gold.'

The Constable made to leave, but Chols stopped him. 'I have a plan. I need some butter and a frying pan!'

That night the townsfolk locked themselves in their houses. Only the mob of armed bakers stood in a quiet line forming a barrier at the bottom of the High Street. Looking up at Malling Hill, they saw the Doughman silhouetted against the moon. He bellowed, then started his galloping stomp down into Lewes. On the other side of the river, the bakers were waiting with their peels, spears and burning torches.

Seeing them, the Doughman bellowed once more and charged. But when he sniffed a whiff of hot melty butter drifting in from the Ouse, he clomped towards it, skidding on the cobbles that lead down to the riverbank.

Chols was floating mid-stream in his 'cart on the water'. He was frying a pan of butter over a small metal stove. Unable to get any closer, the giant clapped his hands, beat his chest and stamped his feet. Chols whistled to the ram. Head down, it butted the monster's crusty ankles. The slipway was so slimy with riverweed and duck poop that the Doughman keeled right over onto his back with his legs poking into the river.

Have you ever thrown a piece of your sandwich into a pond for a duck? If you have, you know that two things happen: first, it goes soggy, and second, one duck rushes over, then another, and before you can say 'Quack, quack, duck snack!' there's a barging crowd of them that seem to have appeared from nowhere.

That's what happened on the slipway that night. The giant's feet went soggy and the ducks rushed in, more following more, until in no time at all they had nibbled and pecked the bread monster clean away. Not even a crumb remained.

When Chols and his ram were summoned
before the Council of Lewes, the whole town
cheered. The important merchants hailed him
as the most public-spirited of all Lewesians
and asked him to become Mayor.

The golden letters of the name 'Leonard
Lardycake' were struck off the list of Mayors
hanging in the Town Hall. Despite that, the
old woman's prediction came true. He was
famous – for being the meanest Mayor the
town has ever known.

Chols never saw the old woman again, but he always remembered her words and became the kindest Mayor in the history of the town. When he retired, he bought an inn at Firle and named it The Ram after his lucky mascot. It's still there now.

Often people who hear this story ask what the Doughman did during that Midwinter's day before returning to his doom. No one really knows, but I suspect he spent his time in Ringmer, just loafing.

* pharisees – in Sussex dialect this means fairies.

13

Seven Sisters and One True Shepherd

◎ The South Downs between Seaford and Eastbourne ◎

When first you beheld me from sorrow I was free
But now you have stolen my poor heart from me.

From 'Shepherd of the Downs' sung
by George Copper, 1784

When the last ice caps dissolved in the south-east, they carved stone and chalk into seven sinuous cliffs curving against the sea between Cuckmere Haven and Birling Gap. These cliffs are called the Seven Sisters, after seven star sisters who used the cliffs as landing pads when they fell from the sky at night, which they did often, so that they could dance high up, looking out across the sea. Their whirling was known to be fast and dangerous. No one ever dared interrupt them as they span in their dizzy circles for hour after enchanted hour.

Until it happened that a kind shepherd who worked the sweeps and folds of the Downs was searching for a lamb in the darkness. One hand rested on his belt which had three buckles. He had made it for himself as a little bit of decoration because he had no mother or sister or wife to embroider his rough linen smock. The other hand rested on his shepherd's crook. He was exhausted and was just about to give up, when he caught sight of the creature at the edge of the cliff called Rough Brow. Throwing his staff to one side, he raced towards it and lunged. Catching hold of its back legs, he grappled its soft middle and saved it from falling.

Panting, the shepherd looked up towards the distant brink of the next cliff, Haven Brow, and saw lights flickering like fireflies threaded on a silver string. Approaching, he saw the lights were woven into the hair of dancing women in dove-white dresses.

They were blowing single notes from bone whistles, each whistle a different pitch, each pitch made by a different woman, who never took the whistle from her mouth. As they span, the dancers beat their feet upon the stones and between whistling, made low grunts and calls with their throats.

The shepherd was drawn like sparks to flint. Six of the women were dancing around a girl with hair as black as the back of a bear and lips as red as rosehips. Although the other dancers flung themselves in wild circles, she swayed slowly from side to side, her cheek on her hand. She seemed tired.

The shepherd stood with his mouth open. The other dancers were too caught up to notice him, but the girl in the middle slowly lifted her head from her hand and smiled. She pointed at him, tapped her chest and nodded. Taking it as a sign that she wanted him to take her away, the shepherd ran forward and, just as he had with the lamb, grabbed hold of the girl by the waist. The six other dancers attacked him with nails and teeth that were like the claws and fangs of wolves, but he put his head down and with the girl under one arm and the lamb under the other, he didn't stop running until he was back on his familiar carpet of downland.

Leaving the lamb with its playmates, he took the girl inside and sat her by the fire in the middle of his hut. He began to pour out hot stew and a stream of words: 'If you want me to take you back I will, but if you want to stay, I'm yours …'

She silenced him with an upraised hand. For three days, she stared: either at the flames or at him. She saw that the shepherd had three stars – three good qualities. The first: he was true. The second: he was kind. The third: he was hard-working. She liked his stars and so, when the three days were up, she spoke.

'I will stay with you. But should you mention my sisters and my dancing even once, I will return where I belong.'

The shepherd swore by every sheep he owned, by the land that he walked and by the crook that he carried, 'I will never mention your sisters, or your dancing.'

She smiled. It was like the first green leaf of spring.

If time were a line of bunting we could abseil down it, and when flags became feathers and ribbons became bones, we'd see for ourselves that from that time to this there has not been a happier man than the shepherd. He was over the moon, he was inside out, not a shred of doubt, not an ounce of fear, he kept her as near as his breath for minutes that seemed hours, days that seemed weeks, weeks that seemed years. It was an eternal summer.

But when the leaves were turning, he woke and she wasn't there. He missed her. The first hour he shrugged it off, the second he split wood, the third he took his shepherd's crook and strode over the Downs, searching. The more he walked, the more frantic he became, breaking through branch and bracken, his staff striking the stone.

When he returned to his hut, jaw set, hair matted with sweat, boots wet with mud, she was there, by the fire.

He howled, 'Where have you been?'

She stood up, arms wide, 'I'm here now!'

'I suppose you've been dancing with those sisters of yours!'

She backed away from him, dried petals flying from her pockets. He covered his face with his hands. After a few seconds, he took them away and whirled round and round in panic. She was gone, not a whiff of her scent, not a whirl of her skirt.

The shepherd picked up his staff and walked to and fro along the seven cliffs that are now known as the Seven Sisters. He walked from

Haven Brow to Short Brow, from Rough Brow to Brass Point, from Brass Point to Flagstaff Brow, from Flagstaff Brow to Bailey's Hill, from Bailey's Hill to Went Hill. Eyes roving, he forgot his sheep, forgot to eat and forgot to drink. Days later, worn out with longing, he fell flat on his back and looked at the night sky. There she was! Unmistakable, shining directly above him, back where she belonged, one of seven stars we call the Pleiades, but once they were called 'The Seven Doves'.

The shepherd sighed one long sigh, connecting earth with heaven.

A body is just a body and when he sighed, the Seventh Sister took him with her to the sky, where he still exists in a line of three stars who are always close to the Pleiades. Three stars for the three buckles on his belt. Three stars for the three things the Seventh Sister loved about him, his kindness, his hard-working nature and his honesty. We know those three stars as Orion's Belt but once the constellation was called 'The True Shepherd'.

14

Duddleswell Woman, the Hare-yWitch

◎ Duddleswell ◎

On the Ashdown Forest, among the tall straight trees and prickly gorse near Duddleswell, a wise woman lived by herself. She knew all the healing qualities of plants and was known to talk to animals. Because she gathered herbs into a long pointy hat to protect their roots, local gossip speculated that she might be a witch. The woman didn't take any notice, she had so many other friends. Foxes with the mange, badgers with snared paws, and frozen hedgehogs who would crawl, limp and stagger to her door, to be released a few weeks later fit and well.

Living in Fairwarp at this time, there was a forester who had two things he loved best in the world: his young daughter and his hunting dogs. He made his living from wood: gathering it, cutting it and burning it into charcoal.

One spring morning, he was out hunting when he saw a big old hare cleaning its ears in the spring sunshine. The forester released his hounds. The hare lifted his head and sprinted.

He bounded across streams, up banks, through gullies, but he couldn't shake off the hounds. A hunting dog will gain an extra spurt when sensing it is about to catch its prey, and as the hare began to flag, the gap between him and the hounds narrowed. Rounding a corner, the hare saw the old woman's hut. With new energy, he surged forward. Still he wasn't fast enough; the leading hound's teeth closed around his left hind leg. Kicking back at the beast's nose with his right leg, the hare managed to free himself and pelt towards safety.

The door opened, the hare ran in and the door closed. The hounds began to bay and the forester banged and bellowed, 'Give back the hare! We won't get another; the hounds are spent!'

There was no answer.

That night the forester could not sleep. At dawn, he pulled on his boots and his hat and set off towards Duddleswell. Anger powered his legs and in no time he was pounding on the door.

It opened instantly. There was the woman. He saw she had fine grey hair and a thin red nose. She was wearing a rough cloak and had a basket on her arm. She looked at him, her eyes as soft as the back of a dormouse. 'We don't get many visitors here. Are you lost?'

'I want to know where my hare is! The one you took away from my hounds yesterday.'

'I expect he's bounding through the forest,' the woman replied. 'He left my house fit and well at sunrise.'

'You lie!' said the forester.

The woman shook her head and walked past him. As she did, the man saw she had a limp. 'It's you! You're limping on your left leg, the same leg that was bitten by my hound. You must have turned yourself into a hare yesterday to cast your spells and work your evil.'

The woman smiled sadly. 'I can't change myself into animals. I'm just an old woman who understands a little bit about herbs and healing. Hare is my friend. He would have died if I hadn't taken his injury on myself.' She lifted up her cloak to show teeth marks on her calf.

At the sight, the man backed away. 'Proof!' he cried.

That night, in the village inn, the forester drank heavily, telling his story to anyone that would listen. 'You should be careful what you say about people,' the landlord shouted through the din.

'Should I?' the forester slurred. 'What if I told you I saw her with my own eyes, turning from a hare back into a woman?' The din fell away into silence.

From that night on, the people of Fairwarp, Maresfield and Duddleswell shunned the wise woman.

A year passed. The forester's precious young daughter caught a winter fever. He spent every penny he had on remedies, medicines and the best doctors from Crowborough to Lewes. They all said the same thing, 'She won't see the end of the week.' The forester couldn't and wouldn't believe it.

As he looked out into the snow he had a thought: 'If only I could take my daughter's sickness on myself.' In that instant, he remembered the wise woman and made a decision. Wrapping his daughter's thin body in thick blankets, he lifted her gently and carried her through the blizzard towards Duddleswell.

To his relief, he saw that smoke was rising from the chimney of the hut. With his foot, he knocked politely. The woman answered and without hesitation ushered him in out of the cold. By the stove a very old hare was sleeping, curled up in a basket stuffed with straw. The woman gestured to the man to put the girl on her bed. He set her down carefully. 'They say she'll die within days. I saw what you did for the hare …'

The wise woman nodded towards the stove. 'That's him there, asleep by the fire. He is old and his time has come. I don't think he'll last out the month. I'll do my best, but your girl's fever looks advanced. The only sure way of saving her would be for another to take on her illness. It's not something I could do myself. As an old woman, the fever would kill me before I'd finished the healing and then we'd both be lost.'

'I want to take on her sickness!' the forester begged.

A series of loud, honking squeaks came from the fire. The old hare had woken up and seemed to be paying attention.

He called again and again. The woman shuffled over, calling back in the same fashion. She stroked his long ears. Turning to the forester she spoke: 'Hare says your daughter needs her father. He'll take on her illness. It's nearly his time.' The forester looked at the hare and then, in shame, at his own feet.

'I don't know what to say.'

'That you won't set your hounds on hares anymore?' the woman answered.

'I won't,' whispered the forester.

Placing the old hare on the girl's chest, the woman burned herbs, wafted smoke and said some words so quietly, the forester couldn't catch what they were.

The hare's breathing slowed as the colour returned to the girl's cheeks. Her eyes opened and she sat up. The wise woman took the animal's limp body and wrapped it in a soft cloth.

The forester and his daughter yomped home through the snowdrifts. By the time they reached their cottage, she was starving hungry and ate a whole apple pie by herself.

Her father ran to the village inn and told everyone that would listen about the kindness of the woman of Duddleswell. For years afterwards he left a pile of firewood outside her hut every week, by way of thanks. He is long gone now, but the wise woman is still sometimes sighted, tending to a fledgling which has fallen from its nest or a fox cub with a cold – not just in Duddleswell but across the forest, 'hare' and there.

A speckled cat and a tame hare
Eat at my hearthstone
And sleep there.

W.B. Yeats

15

Jack and the Devil

◎ Ashdown Forest ◎

Question: What did the nut say
when it sneezed?
Answer: Cashew!

It wasn't the blacksmith's tongs, it wasn't the candle and sieve of Granny Annie, it was young Jack of Alfriston who finally got the better of the Devil – well almost. This is how.

Jack was bouncing on the heather and skimming flint across the grass when he saw an old walnut shell. He picked it up. It had a small hole in the side. Jack looked around and picked up a stick. Would it fit the hole? Nearly. He took out his little penknife and began to sing:

> *There is no if, there is no but,*
> *The stick I'll trim, the stick I'll cut,*
> *See how it fits, see how it shuts?*
> *I've made a nutcase of a nut!*

'That might be useful!' he said and off he tripped, tapping the stick against the nut until the moon rose.

From behind a bush came the Devil. He'd lost his confidence a bit and decided that bullying a little boy might be just the trick to get him back on track.

He shook his horns, stamped his feet and rolled his red eyes.

'Are you scared of me, Jack?'

'Not really,' said the boy.

The Devil puffed himself up till he was as tall as a tree.

'Are you scared of me now, Jack?'

'Nope.'

The Devil blew up his body until he was as tall as Firle Beacon, with red flapping wings, a red forked tail and a red frowning face.

'Are you scared of me now, Jack?'

'Sorry,' shrugged Jack, 'I'm only scared of small things! If you were to make yourself so tiny you could fit in this walnut … well …' he pretended to shiver and opened his eyes as wide as he could get them.

Like a blacksmith's bellows puffing out air, the Devil deflated until he was as small as a caterpillar.

'In here?' he squeaked as he crawled up the side of the walnut.

'Yes.' And once the Devil was safe inside, he said:

There is no if, there is no but,
I've caught the Devil in a nut,
How can I keep him tightly shut?
I'll use my stick to stop him up.

'Done!' he chuckled, as he strolled along, throwing up the walnut shell and catching it.

Jack made straight for St Dunstan. The holy man took a hammer and put the walnut on his anvil.

'Whack!' the nut stayed whole.

St Dunstan took a heavier hammer and with Jack's help to lift it, 'Heave!' he tried again.

'Whack!' it didn't even crack.

This time St Dunstan took a hammer so big he could only lift it with the help of the whole congregation of Mayfield Church.

'Whack!' The nut shattered.

Back then, the people of Sussex rarely shut their mouths. They were either talking, eating or gazing slack-jawed at the clouds, so when the nut split into thousands of fragments, a piece of the Devil flew onto everyone's tongue and was swallowed down.

So, if anyone in this county ever says to you, 'You've got a piece of the Devil in you today!' You can reply, 'It's true and so have you, and this is why.'

And you'll tell them this (forked) tale:

> Bucky, bucky, biddy bean,
> Is the way now fair and clean?
> Is the goose y-gone to nest?
> Is the fox y-gone to rest?
> Shall I come away?

(Traditional spell)